"You okay, man? That was _ _ _ sigh." Dirk gave him a sympathetic look.

"No. No, I'm really not." Logan opened his mouth to spill everything when the newlyweds, Aiden and Dev, walked into the shop. "My godson!"

Dev handed Dylan over without a word, and Logan took him happily. He adored his godson.

Aiden studied Logan. "What's wrong?"

"What do you mean?" He went for innocent.

Aiden raised a single eyebrow, the annoying ass. "Something's wrong. Spill."

"I...." Logan took his coffee and sat, baby Dylan in his arms giving him comfort. "I'm going to foster a set of triplets. They're two days old. I'm supposed to pick them up Monday."

There. He'd said it out loud. He'd gone through the foster-parent classes without telling anyone because he knew he could do this. He could.

Maybe.

Oh God.

WELCOME TO
DREAMSPUN DESIRES

Dear Reader,

Love is the dream. It dazzles us, makes us stronger, and brings us to our knees. Dreamspun Desires tell stories of love featuring your favorite heartwarming heroes, captivating plots, and exotic locations. Stories that make your breath catch and your imagination soar.

In the pages of these wonderful love stories, readers can escape to a world where love conquers all, the tenderness of a first kiss sweeps you away, and your heart pounds at the sight of the one you love.

When you put it all together, you find romance in its truest form.

Love always finds a way.

Elizabeth North

Executive Director
Dreamspinner Press

Sean Michael

THE MORE
THE MERRIER

PUBLISHED BY

Published by
DREAMSPINNER PRESS

5032 Capital Circle SW, Suite 2, PMB# 279,
Tallahassee, FL 32305-7886 USA
www.dreamspinnerpress.com

This is a work of fiction. Names, characters, places, and incidents either
are the product of author imagination or are used fictitiously, and any
resemblance to actual persons, living or dead, business establishments,
events, or locales is entirely coincidental.

The More the Merrier
© 2019 Sean Michael

Cover Art
© 2019 Alexandria Corza
http://www.seeingstatic.com/
Cover content is for illustrative purposes only and any person depicted
on the cover is a model.

Paperback ISBN: 978-1-64108-151-1
Digital ISBN: 978-1-64405-195-5
Library of Congress Control Number: 2018963783
Paperback published June 2019
v. 1.0

Printed in the United States of America
∞
This paper meets the requirements of
ANSI/NISO Z39.48-1992 (Permanence of Paper).

Best-selling author **SEAN MICHAEL** is a maple leaf–loving Canadian who spends hours hiding out in used-book stores. With far more ideas than time, Sean keeps several documents open at all times. From romance to fantasy, paranormal, and sci-fi, Sean is limited only by the need for sleep—and the periodic BeaverTail.

Sean fantasizes about one day retiring on a secluded island populated entirely by horseshoe crabs after inventing a brain-to-computer dictation system. Until then, Sean will continue to write the old-fashioned way.

Website: www.seanmichaelwrites.com

Blog: seanmichaelwrites.blogspot.ca

Facebook: www.facebook.com/SeanMichaelWrites

Twitter: @seanmichael09

Instagram: www.instagram.com/seanmichaelpics

By Sean Michael

DREAMSPUN BEYOND
THE SUPERS
#6 – The Supers
#29 – The Librarian's Ghost

DREAMSPUN DESIRES
THE TEDDY BEAR CLUB
#39 – The Teddy Bear Club
#83 – The More the Merrier

Published by **DREAMSPINNER PRESS**
www.dreamspinnerpress.com

Chapter One

LOGAN trudged through the snow to the Roasty Bean, ready for a hot drink, a sit, and some quality time with his godson, Dylan, and his good friends. His daughter, Sarah, who usually spent alternate weekends with him, was with her grandparents this time, and he was at loose ends. That wouldn't be true for much longer.

Stop it, he told himself. *Be good. Be focused. The guys will… help. Give advice. Something.*

"Logan! Logan, is that you?" Dirk was there, coming up behind him pushing a covered stroller.

"Yeah. Come on. It's cold." He waved and grinned, already feeling better.

Dirk increased his pace, catching up with him easily, and Logan helped the guy maneuver his stroller into the coffeehouse. Little Melinda, Dirk's preschooler, remained fast asleep, not even seeming to notice the switch from cold and damp to beautifully warm. Sweet baby girl.

Zack waved to them from the far side of the counter as the door closed behind them. "Hey, guys! The usual?" he asked.

"Can I have mine with whiskey?" Logan teased.

Zack's eyebrows went up, and Dirk gave him a look. "Has that got something to do with Sarah not being with you today?" Dirk had only been coming to the Teddy Bear Club for a few months, but he'd picked up on the routine pretty quickly. Sarah's school let out early on Fridays, and she was almost always with Logan.

"Nonsense. She's with the grandparents."

"That's good of you—letting them have her on your day. I know how precious time with her is." Dirk pulled the cover away from the stroller to check on Melinda before parking it behind his chair and sitting at the big round table where they met every Tuesday and Friday.

"It's my mom's birthday. They're having a spa day and then a slumber party." Logan went to pay for his coffee. "Where are Dev and Aiden?"

"Apparently Dylan is cutting teeth and being ugly. I told them to come anyway and I'd work my magic on him, so they still may show up." Zack gave him his change.

"Oh, my poor godson!" He grabbed his phone and texted Dev immediately.

bring me my baby boy
you'll be responsible
yep
seriously—teething
bring him
t-e-e-t-h-i-n-g

do eeet He wasn't taking no for an answer.

lol k u asked 4 it

He had. More than anyone understood. God. He shook himself and went over to sit next to Dirk, whose little girl was still asleep. Hopefully she'd wake up before Aiden and Dev arrived because Aiden's Lindsay wasn't going to be happy Sarah wasn't here today—she had a bad case of hero worship going for the older girl. Linds would be even sadder if Melinda was out of commission too.

Dirk gave Logan a warm smile as he took a seat. "I didn't make it on Tuesday," Dirk said, "so I've been looking forward to this all week."

"Yeah? Me too," Logan agreed. "Seriously. I've been busy, but I really needed this today."

"I like that we can come even without the kids, that we get to be teddy bear dads even if we don't have the teddy bears with us." Dirk shook his head. "I'm not sure that came out like I meant it."

"Well, mine is growing up on me, that's for sure."

"I can't imagine Melly being ten. I want to freeze her right where she is. Or maybe take her back to when she was a baby. It feels like forever ago and not long enough at the same time."

"Yeah, I know." Logan sighed deeply, shook his head. God, he needed to talk to the guys. Everything anyone said brought his mind right back to his situation.

"You okay, man? That was a huge sigh." Dirk gave him a sympathetic look.

"No. No, I'm really not." He shocked himself with the admission. He didn't know Dirk all that well. Not like he knew Aiden, Dev, and Zack.

"It didn't seem like you were. What's up?" Dirk sounded honestly curious, and his expression was sympathetic. The guy really was easy to talk to.

"I—" Logan opened his mouth to spill everything when the newlyweds, Aiden and Dev, walked into the shop. "My godson! More teeth!"

Dev looked a little haggard, testament to how badly the teeth-cutting was going. He handed Dylan over without a word, and Logan took him happily. He adored his godson.

Aiden gave him a wry grin. "You want to spend the weekend with us, looking after McFussypants here?"

"You be nice to my baby boy." Logan nuzzled in, enjoying the lovely baby scent and bouncing Dylan easily.

Dev chuckled as Aiden got the girls out of their coats and then carried baby Bee over to the play area while Linds ran to join Zack's twins, Marci and Missi. Melinda woke up at the sound of the other girls squealing, and Dirk grabbed her before she could start crying.

"I play too, Da!"

Goodness, such a pretty girl. Logan loved her dark curls and eyes.

"Of course you can." Dirk set her down again, and she rushed over to her friends. Dirk shook his head. "She always has a tiny moment of panic when she wakes up, but then she's bright and eager. She doesn't even need coffee."

"Everyone needs coffee," Zack, who had come over to join the group, asserted in mock outrage.

Dylan started fussing, and Logan put his knuckle on those sore gums. Dylan had quite a few teeth already, so he had to find the place where the new tooth was coming. It took a moment, but when he found it, Dylan calmed down for him immediately, those big blue eyes gazing up at him.

"Sweet baby boy."

"Everyone seems to have the magic touch but me." Dev looked a little put out, but Logan knew his friend didn't really mind. When Dev had first joined their dad meetings, he'd been on edge from being responsible for his sister's abandoned baby boy. Dylan had clearly picked up on that and been overly fussy with Dev, while Logan and Zack, in particular, were able to calm him. Dev was fine now that he and Aiden were together but occasionally backslid when a minor crisis occurred.

"You're the Jeanette-whisperer." Logan winked at the barista, who was busy filling their orders. "I know you get the best coffees."

Dev grinned. "Is that your way of asking me to go see why your coffee isn't here yet?"

Aiden came back over and studied Logan. "What's wrong?"

"What do you mean?" He went for innocent.

Dirk, Zack, and Dev all turned to look at him, and Aiden snorted. His best friend knew him well.

Aiden raised a single eyebrow, the annoying ass. "Something's wrong. Spill."

"I...." Logan took his coffee and sat, baby Dylan in his arms giving him comfort. "I'm going to foster a set of triplets. They're two days old. I'm supposed to pick them up Monday."

There. He'd said it out loud. He'd gone through the foster-parent classes without telling anyone because he knew he could do this. He could.

Maybe.

Oh God.

All four of them stared at him openmouthed, clearly stunned.

"I-I wanted to foster a kid, maybe a teenager, so I took the classes and finished them Wednesday. They called me this morning." Three newborns—two boys and a girl. He didn't even have a car seat, let alone three, but those babies needed a home, and he was available. Maybe it was meant to be. He'd only just finished the classes, and they'd warned him that it could be months or even years, though it was likely to be sooner. Sooner had won out in a big way.

Aiden pulled himself together first. He came over and hugged Logan tight. "Congratulations! I didn't even know you were looking to foster." Then Aiden laughed, gave him a wink. "I have to tell you, though, three newborns are not a teenager."

"No. No, they're not. I haven't...." He sighed, staring into Aiden's eyes. He'd been as shocked as his friends were now when he got the call for babies instead of an older kid. And so soon after completing the courses and paperwork. "I have no idea what to do."

"Of course you do," Aiden insisted. "You've done this before. And you've got, what? Three days and four friends right here to help you."

His other friends all nodded and made noises of agreement.

"Lists," Dirk suggested. "The first one should be a list of lists. Then you fill them all out, and then you start crossing things off as you do them."

"You're obviously going to be good with newborns," Dev noted, nodding at Dylan fast asleep in his arms. And sure, Dylan wasn't quite a newborn, but he'd only been a few months old when Dev started bringing him to their meetings, and he was still little.

Not as little as newborn triplets, though. Logan didn't know if Dylan had ever been as small as those three.

"You guys should see them. They're beautiful, tiny little redheads." The social worker had texted him a picture. He was pretty sure they'd known that all he needed to do was see them and he'd say yes. Which might have been dirty pool, but the babies clearly needed care. A home. He didn't know the circumstances behind the mother not being able to keep the babies, but they needed immediate care, and the social worker had told him that if his fostering led to adoption, that would work well for everyone all around. Adoption. Him with three babies of his own. It was a reach from expecting to foster an older kid or two, but he wasn't running away screaming from it either.

"You're in love already," Zack accused.

"Who would have thought the big bad lawyer was such a softie?" Dev asked.

"Are you taking time off work?" Dirk wanted to know.

"I'm taking a six-month sabbatical. Then I'll find a nanny, I guess." He wasn't sure if six months would be long enough. Or if he could do without a nanny before then. He imagined he'd find out pretty soon after picking them up.

Aiden gave him another hug, then sat back. "So, what does Sarah think of this development?"

"She loves it. She hates it. She hates me. She loves me." And that had been in the short amount of time that she'd known.

Aiden huffed out a laugh. "That sounds about right."

"So you just had to go and top me, eh?" Zack shook his head. "I have twins, so you go and get triplets."

They all laughed at that, and Dirk pulled a notepad and pen out of the back of his stroller. "What? I like paper for lists. It's more satisfying crossing stuff off than putting in a little tick on an electronic one."

"I.... You guys think I can do this?" Their easy acceptance made him flush with pleasure. The fact that they were all ready to jump in to help reinforced what good friends they were.

"Of course we do." Aiden patted his shoulder. The others all nodded and voiced agreement. "And we've got your back."

"I am going to kick your ass for keeping it all a secret, though," Zack said. "We're your friends, dork."

He didn't have an answer for that, except that he'd thought he'd have time after he finished the courses to bring it up. Who could have guessed they would have tapped him right away? Obviously not him.

"All right. Two and a half days before you have newborn triplets. Let's get these lists made. You have stuff to buy, and some of it has to be in place before those babies show up." Dirk put "list of lists" at the top of the first piece of paper, then wrote "furniture" before turning the page over and writing "furniture" at the top of it. "Crib. You putting them all in one?"

"I don't think I'm supposed to, right? Zack?" Lord, he needed a changing table, clothes, car seats, diapers.... Help. Dirk was right. He needed lists—lots of lists.

"Yeah. They won't all fit in one as they get older anyway."

"So three of everything." Aiden waved at Dirk, who wrote it down, and like that broke the dam, all the guys began calling stuff out, Dirk writing like a man possessed.

"Aiden and I have all the newborn girl and boy clothes you could need. It's all boxed up for charity. It can be yours."

"Thanks, Dev."

Aiden's eyes twinkled. "Not that we can't go shopping for a few new things...."

"Oh, Melly would love to go shopping for baby clothes. In fact, I think she'll be fascinated by the whole baby thing. We'll be able to help you out with childcare," Dirk offered.

Aiden nodded. "You're going to need a lot of support at the beginning."

Dev snorted, making little Dylan jerk in Logan's arms. "And the middle and the end. But you were all here for me. I'm totally going to pass it on."

"I'm happy to help," Aiden added.

"I have to run the Bean," Zack said, "but you know I'll help as much as I can."

"Thank you. All of you." Logan was so scared. Unbelievably. He was giving up his life, his job, possibly his relationship with his daughter, for three babies. Three babies without anyone to love them. There was no way he could have said no. It wouldn't have been right.

"You're a great dad," Aiden reminded him.

"A wonderful goduncle," Dev added.

"And a good man with amazing friends, if one of them does say so himself." Dirk looked at him with a warm smile and admiration in his eyes.

"Well, I.... Okay, let's do this. I'm ready." More ready now than he'd been twenty minutes ago anyway. Their support made a huge difference.

"All right." Zack lifted his coffee mug. "To new beginnings."

"To…." Aiden tilted his head. "Do the babies have names?"

"No." And suddenly he was frozen. Completely frozen.

"Poor wee things. You'll discover their names when you meet them." Dirk patted his hand. "Breathe, okay? We're all here for you. I'll definitely help. Melly loves babies."

"Thank you. All of you." He sat there quite stunned for a moment, but then he took a deep drink of his coffee. "Really. I couldn't tell them no. I couldn't turn them away."

"See? You're a good man. And once you have them, you'll be too busy to worry about anything. Do you want some support when you go pick them up?" Dirk asked.

"What are you going to do? Hire a car?" Dev asked. "Why don't you borrow our van? Dirk, you can drive him." Dev was so sweet. They all were.

"It's spring break so I totally can. And you'll have the car seats by then." Dirk sounded confident about that. "We'll bring Melly—she can fuss over them. What time do you need to be there?"

"At 9:00 a.m. Are you sure? I appreciate it." Logan's hands began to shake. He was really doing this. He didn't know if he was mildly crazy or totally nuts.

Dirk took his hands and squeezed them, warming them. "Hey. You can do this."

"I'm insane."

"Yep." Zack's hands landed on his shoulders, massaging his tight muscles easily. "And a really, really good man."

They all laughed, and that had their girls running over to see what was going on.

"Daddy, why are you holding hands with Mr. Logan?" Melly asked.

Logan hadn't even realized Dirk was still holding on, but he knew it was helping him keep it together.

Dirk answered easily. "I'm helping Logan calm down. He's got three babies coming to him on Monday, and we're going to help him pick them up."

"Babies? Real-life babies?" The little girl's eyes lit up like it was Christmas.

"Yeah, two boys and a girl." Logan opened his phone to the picture of them again and showed it to her.

Melly squealed, the noise happy. "They're so pretty!"

"About time my little Unicorn had some regular boy company here," Dev noted. "He's surrounded by girls."

Aiden snorted. "We still outnumber them, love."

"Oh. Right. I hadn't considered that."

That had them all cracking up.

Maybe. Maybe with the bunch of them, Logan could do this.

Maybe.

Probably.

Maybe.

He hoped.

Chapter Two

DIRK pulled up along the curved driveway of Logan's amazing house, Melly in the nonnewborn car seat in the row directly behind him, watching *Coco* for about the five hundredth time. She could sing along with all the songs and loved the dog beyond all reason. In fact, she had started asking for one, thanks to this movie. It made him smile. Okay, so she made him smile all the time.

The core guys from the Teddy Bear Club had spent the weekend helping Logan get his place babyproofed, along with buying all the stuff Logan was going to need. The lists had been prodigious, but between the five of them, they'd crossed pretty much everything off, and now Logan was equipped with everything from diapers and formula to baby monitors to cribs, changing tables, and baby swings, to a new digital camera for the inevitable masses of pictures he'd want to take. Logan had thanked them all over and over, but frankly, Dirk had been happy to have the excuse to spend more time with Logan. The guy was… special, which his taking in three newborn babies proved. As if he'd needed proof. Logan was the main reason Dirk came to the Teddy Bear Club between classes on Tuesday and why he took Melly out of day care early on Fridays. Oh, he liked all the guys, but Logan was the one who filled his belly with butterflies.

Melly began singing along with another song, her sweet voice breaking him out of his reverie. Right. He had a job to do. Grabbing his phone, Dirk texted Logan to let him know he and Melly had arrived.

Logan appeared and skipped down the stairs, hurrying to the van. Tall and dark-haired, Logan looked gorgeous in his jeans and black turtleneck. He really was a stunner. And he didn't even know it, which only made him hotter in Dirk's opinion. Dirk couldn't help checking Logan out as he climbed into the passenger seat.

"Dirk. My lifesaver. Are you ready to meet them? My babies." Logan was pale as milk, shaking, but along with the worry in his eyes was a light, making them shine. "Rebecca's bringing Sarah over this afternoon after school to get to know them."

"Melly and I are excited to meet them. Does Sarah still love/hate you for agreeing to take them?"

"I did tell her before I said yes, just in case she was totally opposed to the idea. Thank God she wasn't. She's gone through all the emotions since then— excited, scared, mad, happy. It's hard, but…."

"I imagine she'll have times she thinks they're great and times she hates them. Just like most older siblings. Hopefully in the end you'll have a positive balance. That's all any of us can hope for."

"Yeah, I guess so. I never thought, when I agreed to father a baby with Rebecca, that I'd miss out on so much only having Sarah Fridays and alternate weekends."

Dirk took off the parking brake and moved to the end of the driveway before easing out into traffic. "Have you ever thought about asking to have more time with Sarah?"

"At this point, we're leaving it up to Sarah, trying to be flexible. We're both in the same school district, so it's never a problem which one of us she's with on weekdays."

"Ah. I guess I always assumed the fact that you only had her one day a week and alternate weekends was down to an agreement between you and her mother." They stopped at a light and he looked at Logan and gave him an encouraging smile. He thought Logan had a bit more color in his cheeks now.

"Well, in the beginning, yes, but she's getting older, huh? Old enough to have a say. And so far it's been pretty balanced."

"That makes sense. She turns ten soon, right?"

"She just turned ten, yeah. What about your girl? She's going to be four?" Logan smiled back at Melly. "Or is it thirty?"

"Yeah, some days it feels like thirty." He turned off the city street and into the hospital grounds, searching for nonemergency parking. He found it and pulled the van into a spot that wasn't as close to the hospital entrance as he'd have liked. Of course, once they had the babies, Logan could wait inside with them while he brought the van around. It was too cold for newborns to be outside for very long.

Logan took a deep breath as Dirk turned off the engine. "Okay, I think… I think I'm ready for this."

They had the car seats and warm clothes to bring the babies home in, as well as a set of blankets to cover them with, all courtesy of Aiden.

"You are. You've got this." Then Dirk turned to look at Melly. "We're here, Melly. You ready to go see Uncle Logan's babies?"

"Uh-huh. I like to have babies." She held her hands out to him.

"I know." He undid her belts and drew her into his arms, hugging her. He smiled at Logan over her shoulder. "She's going to hate leaving them behind when we go home, I'm sure."

"I really appreciate you helping me. Seriously."

"Well, I'll tell you a secret. I like babies too." Dirk grabbed one of the car seats while Logan took the other two.

"Are we going to keep them, Da?" Melly asked.

"Logan is, honey. We're just helping him with them." He knew Melly would love some baby brothers and/or sisters. She wanted so badly to be a big sister. Anna had died from complications, though, so it wasn't likely to happen. He was just glad he'd won full custody of her when Anna's parents had tried to take her. Thank God the judge hadn't bought their bullshit about his being bi making him some sort of depraved sex maniac.

"Oh." Poor Mel; she sounded so confused.

"I bet Logan will let us come visit lots, though." The man was going to need a lot of help. A lot.

And Dirk wanted to help. He wanted to get to know Logan better. He wanted Logan to get to know him. He'd been attracted from "hello" and had only become more interested the longer he knew the guy. So far he'd liked everything he'd learned about Logan. This was a good man. Someone who was willing to work pro bono; someone who would take on three infants at the drop of a hat.

Logan stopped at the entrance doors and turned to stare at him. "I can do this."

"You totally can." Because whether Logan could or not was irrelevant at this point. He would because he had to. That was how parenthood worked.

Melinda tugged on Logan's sleeve. "I help with babies, Mr. Logan."

God, Dirk loved her. She had the kindest heart, just like her mother.

"Oh, I know you will, sweetie. You're going to be the biggest help ever. Thank you."

He beamed at Logan for that. This was a *very* good man.

"And why don't you call me Uncle Logan instead of Mr. Logan? If that's okay with you, Dirk?"

If anything, his smile intensified. "It totally is."

"Okay, Unca Logan." Melly took Logan's hand. "I help."

"Good deal." Logan took another breath, still holding on to Melly's hand.

An older couple gave them a look as they walked around him and Logan. It was time for them to go inside instead of blocking the entrance.

Dirk took a few steps and triggered the doors, figuring Logan and Melly would follow. "So, are we meeting them at the NICU or the maternity ward?"

"We're meeting at the NICU. I've signed everything, but the social worker is going to meet us up there to make sure things go smoothly."

"Cool." They headed for the elevator, Melly's hand still in Logan's. "Excited?" Dirk certainly was, and they weren't even his kids.

"God yes." Logan laughed, the sound only a little bit hysterical. "Scared, excited, thrilled, panicked. Everything."

The elevator doors opened, and they went in. Logan pressed the button for the fourth floor. He took a few more breaths, and Dirk grabbed his shoulder and squeezed.

"You've got this, Logan."

"I do." Logan nodded a few times, then repeated the words, sounding more confident as he said them again. "I do."

The elevator dinged quietly and the doors slid open. They stepped out, ready to meet Logan's new family.

The social worker was a petite dark-haired woman. She looked tired but happy to see them. Logan shook her hand and introduced Dirk. He shook her hand too. Then she smiled and crooked her finger. "Come see them. The nurses will put them in their car seats for you."

They stopped in front of the windows to the nursery. The curtains were drawn except for over one pane, and behind the glass were three hospital bassinettes that had to be Logan's triplets. The three babies were tiny, with wispy red hair. Faces scrunched up, lips pursed, itty-bitty babies. Two blue blankets, one pink.

Oh God. How gorgeous. Dirk's heart fluttered at the sight of them.

"Da. Look at the babies." Melly sounded awed.

"I know, I see them. Logan, they are so beautiful." Like really, honestly beautiful. Not the beautiful you say because you don't want to insult the parents.

"Yes." Logan made to reach for them, but the glass was in the way, and he pouted. "I want to hold them."

The social worker nodded. "Of course you do. Give me a minute, and we'll get them sorted. You'll be holding your babies in no time."

The three of them watched as the nurses packed the babies up into the car seats, even Melly utterly transfixed the entire time. Two nurses and the social worker each grabbed the handle of a car seat, and for a moment the babies were out of view. Then all of a sudden, they were there, setting the seats down on a couch in a little cluster of seating on the other side of the hallway.

Logan reached down, smiled, and drew a finger along one little boy's face. The baby turned his head, lips open as he searched for a nipple.

"Aww." Dirk reached out and squeezed Logan's shoulder.

"Baby's hungry," Melly informed Logan.

"Do you think so?" Logan smiled down at Melly, then turned to the social worker. "I've got the court order and my ID here for you."

The social worker took his paperwork and examined it carefully. Then she smiled. "Everything's in order, as I expected. You're one of the more organized foster parents I've met. I take it you have everything you need at home?"

"Yes. In triplicate."

She laughed softly, then beamed down at the babies. "I'm happy they're going to a good home. Now, if you want to give them a feed before you go, I do have bottles made up, and there's a quiet room just around the corner you can use." She offered Logan a diaper bag Dirk hadn't noticed earlier.

Logan took it and unzipped it, revealing a half-dozen little bottles of formula, a couple containers of dry formula, diapers, and receiving blankets. It wasn't even close to everything the triplets needed, but it was a nice gesture.

"We probably ought to feed them and make sure everyone is clean and dry before we go home." Logan gave Dirk a blissful look. "I came in last night for feedings. It was lovely."

"Can I feed a baby?" Melly asked.

Logan's expression turned panicked. "Can your da help?"

"I can help. I have to tell you, though, her baby dolls are the best cared for dolls ever." Dirk had no doubt that Melly would not let anything bad happen to any of the three babies while she was around.

"I'm sure. They're just so young."

"And it's your job to worry about them now. I get it. I'm not insulted on my daughter's behalf, I promise."

They made their way to the quiet room beyond the nursery, and Dirk sat on the couch next to Melly.

"They're beautiful. You're a lucky man." He held his arms out and when Logan gave him one of the boys, he let Melly hold him, making sure to keep his own hand there so she couldn't drop him.

Logan managed to hold two babies in one arm—it was a good thing they were so tiny—and fed the little girl first. Look at that, Logan was already being awesome.

Dirk helped Melly get the bottle in her baby's mouth, the little boy latching on immediately, suction strong. "Wow, it looks like they were starving, hmm?"

"Yeah. Yeah, how am I supposed to do this?" Logan asked.

"Looks to me like you already are." Logan would manage because he didn't have another choice, and clearly his instincts were already kicking in.

Logan stuck his tongue out at Dirk, and he chuckled as that set Melly off.

"Daddy! Unca Logan stucked out his tongue!"

"I did indeed." Logan stuck his tongue out again and waggled his eyebrows at Melly.

"Silly Uncle Logan," Dirk teased.

Logan gave him a smile. "Worried Uncle Logan, but you two are making it better."

"What are their names?" Melly asked.

"I'm thinking Samuel, Sebastian, and Susan."

"*S*'s like Sarah," she said. God, his baby girl was smart.

"Very good," Logan exclaimed. "Oh, Mel, you're so smart!"

Dirk beamed at Logan. "She is, isn't she?"

"Babies need burping after bottle, Da," Melly informed him as she pulled the bottle away with a soft popping noise. He looked at the bottle, but he needn't have worried—it was already empty.

"How about you let me do that, sweetie? Real babies are heavier than baby dolls." He took Samuel, or possibly Sebastian, from her and set the boy against his shoulder, rubbing his wee little back. God, holding a baby was a moment of wonder, and this took him right back to when Melly was a newborn. And that newborn smell—it cut right through the antiseptic hospital odor and felt like pure love. A soft hissing noise sounded as his baby didn't burp so much as slowly release the gas in his belly. Melly clapped her approval.

Somehow they managed to get all the babies fed, changed, wrapped up, and back in their car seats. Dirk grabbed a seat in one hand, and Melly's hand in the other, then led the way back down to where they'd come in.

"You want me to bring the van around? They've got a stopping zone to drop off and pick up." That way the babies would stay warm.

"Please."

"I stay and help Unca Logan with my babies."

He glanced up at Logan, who nodded. "Yeah, that's fine."

Taking one last look at the babies and his daughter, Logan standing guard over all four, Dirk took off to where he'd left the van. He didn't run, but he walked faster than he had in a very long time. He almost took a wrong turn with the van, nearly leaving the hospital grounds, but hung a right at the last minute—luckily there hadn't been anyone behind him so he'd been able to cut across two lanes. He pulled up into the loading zone and left the motor running as he sprinted inside to help wrangle car seats.

"They're officially yours now," he told Logan as they went out the doors and into the late winter air. It was snowing far more than any of them cared for at this point. He had precious cargo to transport!

They put all three babies in the very back seat. Logan triple-checked that they were properly locked in as Dirk got Melly clicked in to her much easier to wrangle booster seat.

"Let's go home." Logan looked up at Dirk from the seat next to Melly, having chosen to sit in the back to be closer to the babies. "Let's…. God, be careful."

Dirk checked the road. "It doesn't look that slippery yet. But yeah, I'll be careful."

"Right. I'll order lunch for us when we get to the house. I truly appreciate the help. This would have been really hard to manage on my own."

"It's been our pleasure, hasn't it, Melly?"

"Are we keeping a baby, Da?" she asked.

"No, hon, they are Logan's babies."

"But there's three!" She began to pout. "He doesn't need three whole babies of his own!"

Dirk had to bite back his laughter, and he glanced back at Logan in the rearview mirror to see how he was taking Melly's pronouncement.

"But they need me, don't they?" Logan countered.

Melly scrunched up her nose, clearly considering Logan's words.

"And they'll need you to be their best friend, Mel," Logan added.

Oh, if Dirk hadn't already been interested in Logan, he would be now. As he stopped at a light, he glanced back and beamed at his friend. Logan smiled back.

Then Logan shook his head. "I have triplets and a ten-year-old."

"Yeah. You don't do things by half, do you?" The light changed, and he drove carefully. Luckily Logan didn't live that far away from the hospital, so they should be back before there was much accumulation of snow on the roads. "You're doing it," he said softly.

"I am. Have I lost my mind?"

"Does it matter? You have those babies now—they need you. You have to do it." And Logan could do it. Dirk knew it.

"I do. I will." Logan nodded once, as if that was that.

Dirk kept to five below the speed limit, superconscious of the precious cargo he carried—three little ones, four with his daughter.

"It's insane, isn't it? The pressure."

"It'll ease." Dirk remembered the first week with Melly. He'd been scared to go to sleep in case she stopped breathing.

Of course, Logan wasn't going to be sleeping much at all. Someone was going to have to hire help. Dirk would pitch in where he could—he could tell Melly was going to want to spend a fair amount of time at Logan's anyway, so he wasn't going to be upsetting her by wanting to help Logan out as much as they could.

He pulled up in front of Logan's place, making sure the van's side door was as close to the stairs as possible, then turned off the engine. "Home."

"Home." Logan reached out and squeezed his hand once.

He took a moment to smile at Logan before he got out and opened the side of the van, unclipped Melly, and helped her out. Then he climbed in, grabbed the closest car seat, took it out of its clips, and shut the van door. He went around to the other side to find that Logan was ahead of him, a car seat in each hand. Dirk followed Logan up to the house.

The front door opened before they got to it—Aiden, ushering them in. "I hope you don't mind we let ourselves in."

"Ourselves" turned out to be Aiden and Dev with their kids, Zack and his girls, and Sarah, too, along with a handful of strangers Dirk had never met that he assumed were friends and colleagues of Logan's. The great room also boasted balloons and cake, a table laden with food, and a coffee table full of presents. Logan stood there, looking about as stunned as could be.

Dirk chuckled and patted Logan on the back. "You see? You don't have to do this alone at all. Come on, let's get the triplets uncovered and unwrapped. I think there's about forty people who want their turn at holding a baby. It's a good thing there's three of them."

"At least forty." Logan seemed to shake himself off and headed directly for Sarah, still carrying two car seats. "Hey, baby girl."

"Hi, Daddy. I helped Uncle Aiden plan your party. Do you like it?"

"Oh, you are the best big sister ever. Seriously." Logan handed the babies to Aiden and Dev, who appeared quite insistent about getting their turns first, and drew Sarah into a hug. "I decided you were right about the names, you know."

"They're like mine? They start with *S*'s?" She looked excited about that.

Dirk smiled and held on to Melly's hand as Zack divested him of the car seat he'd been holding.

"That's—Samuel, Sebastian, and Susan."

"So Sammy, Seb, and Suzy?" Sarah suggested.

Dirk chuckled. "You'll never hear their full names again."

"That's the big-sister prerogative, right?" A lovely lady who was obviously Sarah's mother smiled at Logan. "They're lovely. Beautiful."

"Thanks, honey."

Dirk held out his hand. "Hi. I'm Dirk, one of Logan's friends."

"Hello, Dirk. I'm Rebecca, Sarah's mom. So nice to finally meet you!"

Finally? Had Sarah mentioned him or had Logan?

"You've got a lovely daughter," he told her. "Melly wants to be her when she grows up." Sure enough, Melly had let go of his hand and gone right to Sarah's side where she was now talking to Logan.

"Isn't she? I was so lucky that Logan wanted to not only be her donor, but her father. He loves her dearly."

"He does. He's a great father." Dirk could happily sing Logan's praises all day long.

"He is. And would you look at those guys? Wow."

"Yeah, triplets. It's pretty cool, actually." Dirk was sure they would still have been awesome if they'd just been twins, or even a single baby, but the fact that there were three of them did seem to make them extra special. Extra adorable.

"Well, I'm so glad you guys are all here. For him. He needs friends."

That made Dirk chuckle softly. "I have a feeling he'd manage even if we weren't. But happily he won't have to find out."

In fact, he intended to let Logan see that he was there, interested, looking for a relationship. And not because of the triplets. They were a bonus. He offered Rebecca a smile before going to see what was available in the way of munchies. Everything looked great, and he put together a plate to share with Melly and a second plate for Logan. Then he searched for Logan, finding him talking to Aiden and Dev but keeping a sharp eye out for his triplets.

Dirk handed the second plate to Logan. "I figured you might be getting hungry."

"Oh. Thank you. I don't know. I suppose I am."

Dirk chuckled, but he got it. Sometimes you got so wrapped up in what was going on in your life that you forgot little things like food.

"Eat. They're going to need feeding themselves soon enough."

"Can I help feed them, Dad?" Sarah asked, and Logan immediately nodded.

"Of course you can. You'll be a great help."

"Do you have bottles made up here?" Dirk asked. "If not, maybe the girls and I can do that for you."

"Maybe? I don't know. I mean, God knows what the guys have done. There is formula in the kitchen. Clean bottles too."

"Then we'll take care of it." He held out his hands. "Sarah, Melly—you guys want to come help me make up bottles for the babies?"

"Uh-huh. Come on, Sarah. I like the babies." Melly grabbed his hand.

Sarah took his other hand and answered Melly, the two of them chattering happily about babies and feedings and being big sisters.

It was a great start to the triplets' new lives. To Logan and Sarah's new life. Dirk began to whistle as they got to the kitchen, where he found everything they'd need to prep bottles for the babies. A great start indeed.

Chapter Three

EVERYONE was dear and wonderful, but the babies were wearing out. Okay, he was wearing out. Logan wanted to breathe a second, look at the babies. Sort of be in the same space as they were. He wanted to be at home with them and take stock. Hold them and learn them, and nice as this party was, he was eager for everyone to go.

Dirk brought him a glass of water. "How are you doing? Oh wait, don't bother answering that. I can see. Let me talk to Aiden." Dirk went over and murmured into Aiden's ear. Aiden nodded and kissed Dirk's cheek.

His best friend came over and sat next to him, gave him a side hug. "Congratulations on the babies, Logan. They are truly adorable. I mean, seriously. Dev and I are going to get the kids home before all the excitement and sugar turns into wailing and temper tantrums. But even if we're not here, we're thinking of you, and you know all you have to do is call and we'll be right here with whatever you need."

Logan bumped shoulders with Aiden. "I know. Thanks for setting all this up—it's amazing. Especially as I know you didn't have a lot of notice."

"We all make time for friends when they need us." Aiden kissed his cheek. "I mean it. Don't be afraid to call us."

The next thing Logan knew, Aiden had started a mass exodus.

Logan wanted to be a good host, but that would mean getting up and spending who knew how long having goodbye conversations and…. He had triplets.

Triplets.

Three babies.

All at the same time. All tiny and helpless and needing everything from him.

Luckily, Dirk played host for him, thanking everyone and seeing them out, letting him have the luxury of sitting on the couch with his babies in his arms. Even Rebecca had gone, taking Sarah—who'd come over and kissed not only him but all three babies goodbye—with her.

When everyone else was gone, Dirk came back to him. "I'd be happy to clear up for you, but if you'd rather I went too, I can totally go."

He didn't know. He didn't know what he wanted. So in lieu of an answer, he asked, "How's Mel?"

"Sacked out on the couch in your den. Sarah went home with Rebecca." Dirk patted his shoulder. "Why don't you take your babies to bed, and I'll clean up."

"You don't mind if I get them settled?" He felt… like he was in a dream. Nothing else had his attention like the triplets did, but at the same time, they hardly seemed real. Friday morning he'd woken up to a normal, regular day, and now it was Monday afternoon and he had three tiny babies counting on him for everything. Just everything.

"Not at all. In fact, I insist that you do. Go on." Dirk made shooing motions at him, then headed off toward the kitchen, stopping long enough to pick up a few dishes off the dining room table on the way.

Logan turned his attention back to his kids, who were lying side by side next to him on the couch. The boys were both smaller than their sister and darker where Suzy had porcelain skin. They were all perfect, of course. He could already tell Sam from Seb, little Sam's nose not quite as perfect as Seb's. God, they were beautiful.

"Hey, guys. Welcome home. I'm your daddy. I… I promise to love you and take care of you as best I can."

Seb kicked his feet out at Logan's words, but Suzy blew a raspberry at him, and Sam simply snored.

"Right. Focus." He got the boys side by side in one arm and managed to pick Suzy up from the couch in the other. It was scary as hell walking to the staircase, then up the stairs, but the babies were safely in his arms, and he took it slowly so he didn't trip going up. The whole way, two pairs of blue eyes gazed up at him. He wondered what color they would end up being, but for now that blue was stunning.

The door to the nursery was open, the inviting yellow paint bright and cheerful. One wall had a little pastoral scene painted onto it—a field with sheep and cows and a bunch of wildflowers dotting the green for color. There was a rainbow across the sky. Rebecca had outdone herself, getting that accomplished in the short time she'd had.

Suzy whimpered, bringing his attention immediately back to the babes in his arms. He was pretty sure she needed a new diaper, Seb needed a sock put back on, and Sam was still fast asleep. He put them together in the crib closest to the changing table, then grabbed Suzy and made short work of her very soggy diaper. He changed her out of the onesie from the hospital, putting her in pink pajamas with little fold-overs on both the arms and the legs, then wrapped her in a flannel receiving blanket that had come out of the dryer that morning. He set her in her own crib, then grabbed Seb and put him in a matching but green pair of pajamas. He swaddled Seb and stuck him in the second crib. Sam was next, and he didn't wake up during the change, nor when he was wrapped and set in the final crib.

Logan spent a long time staring down at them, only moving away when both Seb and Suzy had joined their brother in dreamland. Even then he didn't go far, moving to sit in one of the glider chairs so he could continue to watch them.

He didn't have a clue how long he'd been doing that when Dirk popped his head into the room. "Hey, the leftover food is all in the fridge, and the place is picked up, more or less."

"You want to sit for a second?" he whispered. He owed Dirk a lot, the least of which was a few minutes of companionship as the babies slept.

"Yeah? You're up to a little more company?" Dirk came and sat in the second chair, rocking gently as he looked at the triplets.

"Yeah. Yeah, I just… it was loud. I was getting… overwhelmed." There had been a lot of people in his house, and though it was big and they were all his friends, they'd all wanted to talk to him and coo over the babies. And hold them. Logan hadn't even had a chance to hold them for that long yet.

"Hey, four hours is more than enough partying for someone who has had newborn triplets for all of an hour."

"Thank you." He reached out like he was going to take Dirk's hand.

Dirk met him halfway and grabbed his fingers, squeezed. "You're welcome." Dirk's fingers slid from his.

Okay, that wasn't awkward. He let himself rock, eyes on those three swaddled doll babies.

"They're beautiful. I know it seems overwhelming right now, but you're a very lucky man. And it'll get easier as you get used to it," Dirk promised him.

"Oh, it's not like I haven't done this. I just didn't do it full-time, and I didn't do it with three." But he was as ready as he could be—he couldn't have said no even if he wasn't ready. The minute he'd seen their picture, he'd known these babies needed him.

"You going to miss lawyering?" Dirk asked.

"I'm sure I'll have some things to do from the house. I'm looking forward to being more hands-off, though." He wanted to enjoy his new family, give them every advantage. He had a couple of junior partners now, and he was pretty sure they could handle most things on their own.

"I'm so pleased for you." Dirk went from looking at the babies to smiling at him. "And I mean it about wanting to help out. If you don't lean on me and Melly, we'll both have words for you."

"I know you're a busy man, that you have a life." The offer meant so much, though. More than Logan could say.

"There's only another three months of school left, and Melly loves babies, so you'd be doing us a favor, really."

He didn't believe that, but it was sweet of Dirk to say so.

He had this huge house, and it was empty except for every other weekend. He'd inherited it, along with a good-sized trust. Add to that his work, and he was more than set. But six bedrooms? Seven baths? What was he doing here? He could have taken in sextuplets and still had more room than they needed. Good grief. Sextuplets. He couldn't even imagine. Just thinking about it made him feel a little green around the gills.

"Hey." Dirk's hand landed on his thigh and squeezed gently. "It's going to be okay. Really."

"I hope so. I'm ready." Not for sextuplets, but he could do triplets. Funnily enough, three seemed far more manageable now that he'd imagined having six.

"Good. Because they're going to be up soon, all wanting to be fed." Dirk grinned. "If you want us to stay, we can, but if you want your first night on your own, I totally get that and won't be offended if you kick us out, I promise."

"Well, let me at least give you and Melly a room, a real bed."

"That would be great, actually. That way you can get help in the middle of the night, and I won't feel like I abandoned you."

"And I wouldn't feel so much like I was putting you out." He didn't have it together anymore, and he knew it. Now that the babies were here, his carefully ordered life was going to be crazy. He'd have to deal with that or let it make him nuts, and he knew he couldn't afford to be nuts until the triplets were old enough to leave home.

"You aren't putting me out. I volunteered, you didn't ask, remember? I think you're going to need to stop worrying when people offer to help, trust that they mean it, and accept every single offer as it comes in."

"Right? You're absolutely right." He shook his head, grinned.

"If folks don't want to help, they won't offer, I would think." Dirk shrugged. "And if they do and don't mean it, well lesson learned for them to not offer what they're not willing to follow through on."

"I think you're right." He stood, taking a last look at the babies. "Come on, let's choose a room for Melly."

"A whole room just for her?" Dirk laughed softly. "How many bedrooms do you have?"

"Six." Not including Sarah's attic getaway.

"Honestly?" Dirk shook his head. "Okay, then. She can totally have a room for herself. I guess I get one too. If you've got beds in all of them."

"I do. It's an old house."

"Very cool. Should we help ourselves, or did you want to show us around?" Dirk asked.

"I'll show you around and let you decide, huh? I inherited. It's been in my family for generations." He always felt a little strange showing people around what amounted to a mansion, given that he was one man with a daughter who only stayed here part-time. Of course, that wasn't true anymore. Now there were three new little lives filling the space, helping turn it into a proper home.

"That's pretty cool, man." Dirk followed him out of the triplets' room, and Logan left them alone for the first time since he'd gotten them.

That wasn't freaking him out at all. Nope, not him. He reminded himself that he could hear them along the hall should they start making a fuss and crying. If he kept saying it over and over to himself, he wouldn't have time to worry. The only reason he didn't turn right around and go back to check on them was because Dirk was there, and he knew he'd feel like a paranoid idiot if he had to explain it to his friend.

Logan cleared his throat and made himself focus on what he was doing. "This is the master, and there are three bedrooms here—one was Sarah's until she moved to the garret. Then there's another suite in the other wing, along with another bedroom." The place was ridiculously large for just him and Sarah, only slightly less so when he added the triplets if he was honest. But there would be rooms for each of them when they graduated to that, all close to him and each other.

"Melly and I can sleep in one of the three bedrooms. If you've got a double bed in one of them, we can take that."

"Sarah's old bedroom is set up for a princess—Melly might like that." Sarah had wanted more grown-up decor when she'd moved into the neat space in the garret. They'd had a great time shopping for the room.

Dirk lit up at that. "That actually sounds great. Show me which one, and I'll carry her up."

"Of course. Come on." The princess room was next to the nursery. He opened it up, revealing it in all its pink and sparkly glory. There were even several posters of unicorns gracing the walls. It screamed girl in the most traditional of ways, but it had been what Sarah wanted when she'd been younger.

"Oh, this is adorable. Melly's going to want her own room done up like this."

"She can stay here anytime."

"I guess that means I can too, eh?" Dirk gave him a half smile, eyes twinkling.

"You can, yes. Of course. There's plenty of room." Not in this bedroom, because the little princess bed wouldn't fit Dirk, but there were plenty of rooms in the house. Plenty.

"We might just take you up on that a lot. Our place is much smaller and doesn't have adorable babies."

"Where do you live?" Logan had never been to Dirk's place, so he had no clue where or how small the place was.

"I've got an apartment in the buildings at the corner of James and Hawthorne."

Oh, that wasn't the best neighborhood at all, but the rent was no doubt commensurate with what a teacher brought home, especially after day-care costs. Still, damn. He didn't like the thought of Dirk and Mel living in that neighborhood. At all.

"I've been living here on and off since I was a little boy." The family home was just that, his great-great— or something like that—grandfather having built it for his family of twelve. It was hard to believe that out of all those relatives only he and Sarah were left, but most of those twelve had died childless.

Dirk interrupted his thoughts. "That's really cool. I like a place with some history."

"Yeah? Me too. Although I get a little rattle-y in here all by myself," he admitted. "It's so empty, but it's mine."

Dirk grinned at him, looking delighted. "It's not going to be empty anymore. You've got those babies to help you fill the spaces."

"You know it. Why have all this wonderful space if you can't share it?" He hoped his kids would make wonderful memories here.

Dirk moved in for a hug. He smelled good. "Thanks for letting us stay. Are you going to be able to get any sleep tonight?"

"I don't know. I really appreciate you hanging out with me, though. I'm wired for sound." And that was the truth. Logan hugged Dirk tight, loath to let go.

"I've got your back, man." Dirk petted his back as if to illustrate his words, the touch gentle.

"Come have a cup of cocoa? We can take it to the master, if you want. There's a sitting area with a fireplace. And a large television." He spent a lot of time there when he couldn't sleep. He supposed now he wouldn't have to worry about what to do in the middle of the night—there were three mouths that were sure to need filling and three little bottoms with diapers in frequent need of changing.

"That sounds amazing, actually. Let me get Melly up into bed in the princess bedroom, and then I'm all yours."

"I'll make the cocoa." Logan followed Dirk downstairs, breaking off to go to the kitchen while Dirk headed toward the den. Look at him, not even checking on the babies, proving both they and he could be all right even if he wasn't watching over them every single second.

Logan hummed as he heated some milk on the stove, then added some hot-chocolate mix to it. He found an unopened package of mini marshmallows in the cupboard next to the fridge and added a half dozen to both mugs. He grabbed a small plate when he found a lovely stash of cookies on a tray from the party and put a couple of each onto the plate, filling it up. Perfect.

He was pouring the hot drink into the prepared mugs when Dirk joined him in the kitchen.

"She didn't even wake up." Dirk sounded pleased about that.

"Oh, that's good. Those babies sure did fascinate her."

"They did. I think we're going to be here a lot because if not, she's going to talk me into getting triplets of our own." Dirk shook his head, but he was smiling.

"Oh lord. You can share with me, huh?" The more he said it, the more he liked the idea of not being on his own for this journey.

"That works for me. I do not have room for triplets. Hell, I don't think I have room for one more." Dirk chuckled. "You, on the other hand, have a gloomy old mansion."

"Gloomy?" Was it gloomy in here?

"Well, gloomy was a bit dark, maybe. Empty? Either way probably not much longer. Those babies will turn it into a home, eh?" Dirk took his cocoa. "Oh, you found the cookies. Cool."

"I did. Everyone was so generous. You should see what Sarah's done to the garret. It's an explosion of tween joy." Purple and glitter and flowers and ribbons and banners. Posters. It suited Sarah down to the bone.

"Maybe she'll show it to me next time we're both here," Dirk suggested.

Logan appreciated that, Dirk not assuming that they could go look now but waiting for it to be Sarah to show him. The guy had great instincts when it came to kids. "I'm sure she will. She's very proud of it."

"Cool." Dirk followed him up the stairs. "Though I have to admit, I'm looking more forward to seeing your room than Sarah's."

"Well, come on. It's where I live." He led Dirk down the hallway. Both doors to the kids' rooms were open, and he peeked in. Everyone was still asleep— babies and little girl. He had a monitor for the babies, but he'd bet with all the doors open, they'd hear the triplets and Mel if any of them woke up.

They made their way to his bedroom, which was huge. It was the original master suite and was furnished as a bedroom at one end and a sitting room at the other. A pair of love seats faced the fireplace, with the television mounted above it, while the heavy four-poster bed and accompanying bedside tables were at the back of the room, the doors to the closet and the en suite there as well. He'd painted the room white years ago to lighten it up. Maybe gloomy wasn't the worst adjective for the place, given all the dark wood and wallpaper in other rooms. He was trying to turn that around. There was just too much to do to tackle more than one room at a time as he needed them.

"Oh wow. You really can just live up here, can't you? Aside from forays to the kitchen, of course. It's really warm and inviting." Dirk looked around, smiling.

"It is. It's a good space. My office is downstairs, and it's been redone as well." It was next to the den, which would work out well as the kids got older. He could keep their toys there. The TV and all the kiddie movies were already down there, along with the Apple TV so they could stream stuff from Netflix and the like.

"Very cool. Is the fire gas or the old-fashioned wood and flame variety?" Dirk moved to sit on one of the love seats.

"This one is gas. It's easier to quench. The huge one in the ballroom is wood."

"So, it's not a problem to have this one on tonight?" Dirk looked yearningly at the fire. "I do love watching the flames."

"Of course not. It helps take the chill off too." Logan grabbed the remote and turned it on.

"Oh, that's nice." Dirk shifted, leaning against the back of the love seat, and took a sip of his cocoa. "Mmm. Perfect. What a lovely spot to unwind."

"Isn't it? We have music, movies, whatever. And, of course, the fire and comfy seats." He loved it in here. It was home.

"This feels lived-in, comfy and cozy. I can see why you focused on this space given how big the rest of the place is. I hope you have someone come in every now and then and dust all those rooms. I'd hate to have to do a place this big all by myself."

"Once a week. I'm not all into having a staff per se." He wanted his kids to have a relatively normal life, but who wanted to spend hours to keep the place tidy? Not him. Sarah was in charge of her own room, but for the rest of the place, a maid just made sense.

"Yeah, well, this place is so huge you'd be cleaning constantly if you didn't have someone come in once in a while."

He laughed at how Dirk's thoughts had gone in the same direction as his own. "Exactly. I need someone to do the floors."

Dirk chuckled, seeming somehow tickled by his words.

"I can't believe this happened. I thought I'd have a few older kids coming for a short stay, then leaving again," Logan admitted.

"Would you have preferred that?" Dirk asked.

"No. No, I was hoping for a family. I mean, I have Sarah, don't misunderstand me, but I don't get to see her often enough. They'd just warned me things didn't usually move very fast in the adoption world and that often older kids need a place to stay on a temporary basis while their home situation is being figured out."

"Yeah, I've always thought not having Sarah around more often had to suck for you. Well, I'm glad you got the family you were hoping for instead of the come-and-go kids like you were expecting."

"I am too. I always wanted a big family, a husband, the whole thing. I thought it would come easy. I was wrong." He just had to work at it. No big deal. He was smart. And fate certainly seemed to be on his side now too. Maybe he'd needed to do something like the adoption process in order to let the universe know he was truly ready.

"Everything looks easy when you're nineteen, doesn't it?" Dirk chuckled. "It seems less easy the older you get."

"You know it. At nineteen the world is brand-new. By now, it's a little dusty."

"Yeah, but at nineteen we wouldn't have appreciated the things the dust has settled on." Dirk crossed his eyes. "I think I'm torturing this metaphor to death, but hopefully you got what I meant."

Logan began to laugh, tickled pink.

Sitting back, Dirk laughed too, then drank some more of his hot cocoa. "This was just what the doctor ordered."

"It i—"

One baby began to wail, and then there were immediate answers from the other two.

Dirk offered him a smile and said, "I'll give you a hand?"

"Please?" He put down his mug and all but ran to the nursery where he fell in love all over again with three bright red, angry little bundles. "Hey. Hey, guys. It's okay. Daddy's here." He rubbed their bellies, all of them calming a little at his touch. And wasn't that the most amazing thing ever?

Dirk was along in moments, carrying three bottles with him. He passed two of them over to Logan as Dirk grabbed little Suzy, cradling her and putting the bottle to her lips. "Oh, look at her. Such a hungry little girl."

Logan let the other two eat in their cribs, holding a bottle in each hand. He was going to have to figure this out. Somehow.

Dirk was singing and cooing at the baby girl in his arms, the smile on his face stunning. He looked about as happy as Logan had ever seen him.

"You're good with babies," Logan murmured.

"I like little kids. They don't judge, you know?" Dirk might have been answering him, but all his attention was on Suzy, tone of voice soft and easy.

"No. No, they just need the basics—warm, dry, fed, and loved."

"Yeah." Dirk turned her over carefully so she was belly down along his arm and rubbed her back until a huge burp came out of her, making Dirk giggle softly. Then he sat back with her and rocked in the glider.

Logan picked both his boys up once they'd fed and sat next to Dirk. He burped one on each knee, cleaning up the spit-up from one.

"You're going to be a dab hand at that in no time. Actually, you're already doing pretty good," Dirk noted. "The real trick will be if you can you do it with all three of them. You think that's possible?"

"No. No, I imagine I'll need to hire full-time help, and soon." He wasn't sure he wanted to—his initial plan had been to hire help in six months or so when he started to work again—but that wasn't an option now. He'd known three would be a lot of work, but he was pretty sure they were going to be enough work that he needed help now.

"If I wasn't working, I would totally help you out. I can't imagine anything more rewarding than helping to bring these sweet little beauties up." Dirk really did look happy and peaceful.

"I'm sure I can find a nice nanny. Or two. Maybe three once I'm back to work." Oh, he was going to throw up, the whole thing suddenly, and utterly, overwhelming, starting with having strangers dealing with his children while he wasn't here.

Dirk simply looked at Logan and blinked for a moment. Then Dirk shook his head. "How about you don't worry about that for now? You've got me for the rest of the week, and that gives you time to get someone in and know for sure how much help you're going to need. Right now you need to breathe before the babies pick up that you're panicking." Dirk had clearly read Logan's mood on his face because he was bang on.

"Right. Right. No panicking." On cue, one of the boys began to scream, and he realized he wasn't sure which one it was.

Dirk handed Suzy over to him and plucked the unhappy baby out of his arms at the same time. Standing, Dirk danced slowly with the little one, bouncing him.

"Shh. Shh. It's okay, sweet baby boy. We'll figure out what's wrong. Is your tummy sore?" Shifting him, Dirk rubbed his tummy. "Sometimes they're allergic to certain kinds of formula."

The baby quieted quickly, though, snuggling into Dirk's arms, and Logan knew it was him. He was nervous, so they were nervous.

"Not colic or allergies to the formula. Just a little fussy. Yeah. Dodged a bullet there." Dirk kept bouncing and rubbing the baby's belly.

"I am going to be great when they start arguing." He was a lawyer, after all. Of course that wasn't going to be for ages. He needed to be good with them now.

Dirk laughed softly, the sound gentle and comforting somehow.

"I'm a little scared," Logan admitted, his gut telling him Dirk wouldn't judge him too harshly for it....

"I think I'd worry more about you if you weren't." Dirk put his sweet baby boy in one of the cribs and came to sit next to him, arm going around his shoulders. "What can I do to help?"

"You're being more help than I can say. I'm being a twat."

"Nah, that's not true. You're totally allowed to be freaked-out. Three babies at once. I was pretty freaked-out with just one when I had Melly."

"Yeah. Yeah. I was taken aback a little." A lot. He'd tried very hard not to let the freaking out happen in his conscious mind, but reality was hitting him right now. He wasn't sure what he'd have done if Dirk hadn't been here with him.

"You're going to be fine. Just fine. Anytime you need to hear that you've got this, that you can do it, you give me a call and I'll be happy to tell you." Dirk squeezed his shoulder. "Every new parent goes through this. I know you've already got Sarah, but this is entirely different. Three babies at once. You can do it, but you're going to need to make some adjustments, that's all." Was Dirk talking to him in that same calm, soft voice he'd used on the babies moments ago?

It didn't matter; the words were helping. He took a breath. "Right. Exactly." He checked diapers and tucked babies back in to their cribs. They were so tiny in them, it made him wonder if he shouldn't just start them out in one together. They might be happier together.

"See? You're doing great. We're going to be able to go back to your room and watch a movie or something like originally planned. This was a need for feeding, nothing huge or terrible."

"I'd love that. Thank you so much, Dirk." He grabbed his friend and held on. "Seriously."

Dirk wrapped his arms around Logan and gave him a warm, tight hug.

God, that felt good. Logan let himself lean, hard. Dirk didn't complain or back off. The guy simply let him lean and offered support. He thought again that he wasn't sure how he'd be getting through this first day without Dirk here. Finally he backed away, and they headed back into his bedroom. Movies. Rest. Friendship. The good stuff.

And if he leaned on Dirk during the entire movie, well, neither of them had a problem with that.

Chapter Four

DIRK packed for Melly and himself and got her settled in her car seat in his Yaris to head for Logan's. He'd spent the better part of spring break hanging out with Logan and the babies, making the occasional outing with Melly. They'd seen a couple of movies and gone to the park a few times, but she'd been utterly fascinated with the babies and had been very patient with them. Which was just as well as that's where they were headed now, for the weekend.

He'd called Logan every day after work, the guy sounding more and more tired as the week passed. After talking to him today, Dirk had decided that he and Melly needed to go back to Logan's for the weekend. He thought Logan could probably use a full night's sleep or two and was more than willing to help him get it by taking care of the babies.

He supposed he wasn't surprised, really, that Logan was having trouble finding help. Three babies were a lot. Of course, he and Melly were perfectly happy to help, and they weren't even getting paid. So maybe it was simply a matter of Logan needing to find the right person. Someone who loved babies and knew how to take care of them. If Logan got some sleep and some help, Dirk was pretty sure he wouldn't feel so overwhelmed. Logan had mentioned someone starting today, so he hoped that was going well.

After pulling up into the circular drive of Logan's place, Dirk turned off the engine and looked in the back to smile at his girl. "You looking forward to spending the weekend with Uncle Logan and the babies?" He wasn't sure if Sarah was going to be there or not—she hadn't been last weekend, but that had been Rebecca's weekend. This was technically Logan's, but Dirk didn't know if Logan was still having Sarah on weekends at the moment, or if Rebecca was keeping her until Logan had taking care of the triplets under control.

"Yes! My babies!" Melly jumped around on the driveway as soon as he let her out of her car seat.

Laughing, he took her backpack and helped her put it on. Then he grabbed his bag, and they headed up the front steps. He knocked gently—no reason to wake the babies if they were sleeping.

Sarah opened the door, tears on her cheeks. "Daddy's firing the nanny. She slapped me."

Holy shit, that was not on. He went down on one knee and opened his arms. She flew into them, crying on his shoulder. He hugged her while Melly patted her back. "That's a terrible thing to do. If your daddy had known she would do that, he would never have hired her." Jesus, and this was someone who had had references? Who worked with kids on a regular basis? Dirk knew Logan wouldn't have hired her otherwise, and he was shocked this had happened.

"I told Daddy I'd come and stay and help if he needed me to," Sarah managed through her tears.

"That's because you're a wonderful big sister." He kissed the top of her head. "Come on. Let's go to the kitchen and see what we can have as a snack while your daddy gets rid of the very bad nanny." He couldn't imagine what Sarah could have possibly done to warrant a slap. She was a good-hearted little girl, and Melly adored her. Hell, even if she'd been rotten to the nanny, it wouldn't have warranted a slap.

"Okay. Come on, Melly. You want a cup of milk?" Sarah took Melly's hand and then took Dirk's with her other. "I'm glad it was you at the door, Uncle Dirk."

"I'm glad it was me too." He could hear voices from Logan's office, but he ignored them. He would keep the girls in the kitchen until the nanny who'd hit Sarah was gone.

He almost—almost, mind you—felt sorry for the woman. Logan could be vicious. There was a reason he was a great lawyer. She was going to be lucky if she didn't find herself sued. What he wanted to do was go in there and slap her and ask her how she liked it.

He pushed his anger away and focused on the girls. Logan was dealing with the slap-happy nanny; he would deal with Sarah's hurt. "So, what sounds good for a snack? Peanut butter and jam sandwiches?"

It seemed that Sarah approved. "That sounds good. Can I have strawberry jam with mine, please?"

"You both can." Because as soon as Sarah had asked for strawberry jam, that would be what Melly wanted, or he didn't know his little girl. "You can get the jam out for me, please. And Melly, can you get the bread?" It was in the breadbox on the counter, which Melly could reach with the help of the little stool kept in the corner. Dirk was willing to bet that was for Sarah, even if she didn't need it as much anymore. He grabbed a knife, four plates, and the peanut butter. Melly very carefully opened the package of bread and put two pieces of bread on each plate.

"Get the fuck out before I have you arrested!" The front door slammed, and then the babies started to cry. Logan called out, "Sarah, are you okay?"

"Uncle Dirk is here, Daddy. We're having a snack."

Oh man, those babies were not going to settle as upset as Logan was. Sure enough, the man looked into the kitchen to check on Sarah first, his face like a thundercloud.

"Why don't you help with the sandwiches and I'll get the babies to settle real quick," Dirk suggested. He patted Logan on the shoulder and went to the living room, where the babies were in their little bouncy seats. He was betting they'd been startled awake by the door slamming, or possibly the yelling, and it wouldn't take much to settle them down again if he remained calm.

They kicked and screamed when they saw him, demanding his attention.

"Hey, hey, little ones. Did you miss me?" Did they recognize him already, this early? He couldn't remember how it had been with Melly. He picked Sam up and put the little guy over his shoulder while he made the other two's chairs bounce lightly. "Sorry for the noise. Your daddy's trying to get everyone settled and organized, you know? You'll have a routine soon enough. You really will."

They calmed quickly, all three of them more than ready to return to their interrupted nap time. Thank goodness for that—he was pretty sure he was needed in the kitchen. He set Sam back down in his chair without waking him and quietly made his way back to the kitchen.

Logan was sitting with Melly in his lap, one arm around Sarah. Oh. Oh, that was a sight to melt his heart. He stopped in the doorway and simply watched for a long moment, soaking it in. It made him yearn for more moments like this, for this to be his reality on more than just some weekends.

Then he took a breath and walked in. "How are those PB&Js coming along?"

"We were having a hug first, Da. Unca Logan is having a rough day." Melly sounded so grown-up.

"Hugs are even better for rough days than peanut butter sandwiches. Can I join in the hugging?"

"Of course, Da!" Melly held one of her arms out for him.

He went to his knees and wrapped his arms around all of them.

How natural, how easy this felt. He stayed right there with them, all four of them breathing together. Logan looked so tired, so worn-out. He needed some serious help. Someone who wasn't going to solve problems with hitting. If she'd done that to Sarah, God only knew what she would have done to the triplets if they were having a bad day.

His knees weren't too happy with him, given the hard tile of the kitchen floor, so Dirk stood. "Okay. Sandwiches all around."

"Peanut butter!" Melly called out. "Can I take my backpack to my room, Da?"

"Go ahead, Melly." He tousled her hair. She had a room here that she considered hers. He liked that. He loved that Logan had given that to her.

She climbed down from Logan's lap and ran off, and he called after her, "You leave the babies alone. They're sleeping."

He could almost hear her sigh, but he trusted she would do as she'd been told. He started putting together a sandwich for each of them. "Are you two okay?"

"That woman… seriously? Who raises a hand to a…? I mean, Jesus." Logan grabbed Sarah and held her tight. "I'm so sorry, baby."

"'S'okay, Daddy. She didn't hit the babies, did she?"

Sweet big sister looking out for her new siblings. It made Dirk smile as he added the jam to the sandwiches.

"No." There was a darkness in Logan's voice. "In fact, I'm going to call that service right now. I don't suppose you have a brother who wants to be a manny, Dirk?"

"Nope. I was an only child. You know, Melly and I would be happy to help out until you can find someone. I have school from eight till two, but I could be here outside of that, and summer holidays are just around the corner." He hoped that hadn't been too forward, but it was an honest offer. He really liked Logan, and who wouldn't be in love on sight with those three beautiful babies? Melly certainly adored them, so he knew she wouldn't mind spending more time here.

"Yeah? We might have to discuss that. I have all this house…." Logan stood. "I am going to call that service, though. Right now."

Dirk nodded. "Yeah, that kind of behavior doesn't stand. I'd hate to think of her doing that to any kid.

Your sandwich is ready when you're done." He put the plates on the table, setting one in front of Sarah and one where he was going to sit.

"Are you going to come stay? Really?" Sarah asked.

He had to admit, he lived in a barely adequate space. This house was fabulous and Melly already had a room that she thought of as hers. And if he was being really honest, he adored Logan. Okay, he was kind of in love with the guy. He'd been wanting to get closer to Logan almost from their first meeting, and everything he'd learned about Logan since had only made him like the guy more.

"Your father and I have to talk about it some more, but we might. Would you like that?" It would suck if she didn't want him and Melly here more often.

"Daddy needs a friend. It would be neat, to have a big family here."

She really was a darling.

"It feels like it needs a big family, doesn't it?" He grabbed some glasses and poured Sarah and himself each some milk. Then he sat next to her.

"Uh-huh. You know that my mom and dad never were married or in love or anything? They're both gay. They just wanted me." She sounded so grown-up, the way she said it.

"Yeah, I know. That's pretty wonderful, isn't it? Having someone want you so much they made you special."

She shrugged. "It can be a little weird, but it's not bad, and now I have brothers and a sister and a Melly."

"You do indeed." He put his arm around her and gave her a hug. "You're pretty lucky."

"Yeah. You know, Melly's been gone a while…."

"Yeah, I was just thinking the same thing." She had probably been distracted by the babies, but at least it sounded like she hadn't woken them. "Should we go look for her?" He was never going to get to eat his sandwich.

"Uh-huh. Then sandwich?" Sarah suggested.

They headed to the open living room and found Melly with a blanket and a pillow, lying next to the babies, sound asleep. Oh damn. His heart melted again. Totally and completely. He swallowed hard.

A warm hand landed on his shoulder, Logan murmuring, "She's watching her babies."

"She is indeed. They've got quite the fierce protector there." He turned to smile at Logan. "Come on. Sarah and I are starving, and I bet you are too."

"Yeah. She's fine. We'll hear her on the monitor."

"Yeah." He hadn't been watching because he was worried, but because he was enchanted. That was okay, though.

They trooped back to the kitchen, he poured a glass of milk for Logan, and they all sat to finally have their late afternoon snack.

Sarah chatted happily to them about school and about her day and her teachers, the sound comfortable, homey. Looked like she hadn't been traumatized by the slap. Thank God.

"I think we should totally order fried chicken and mashed potatoes for supper." Logan grinned as Sarah bounced at his suggestion.

Dirk loved how it always seemed that as one finished one meal, the next was planned. "That sounds yummy. Is that your favorite, Sarah?"

She nodded and rubbed her tummy.

Chuckling, he gave Logan a grin. "Yours too, eh?"

"I do like food that's bad for you."

"Only on Friday," Sarah said solemnly.

"I like it." And he'd like to be a part of that tradition on a regular basis. He figured now, with the babies and Melly still asleep, was a good time to jump right in. "So, were you serious about me and Melly moving in?"

"There's room, you know, and... it's a good house. We're a good family, right, Sarah?"

"Uh-huh. With brothers and sister and Melly." It looked like Sarah had already accepted Melly as a part of her family, moved in or not.

"It would sure beat living in my little apartment. And then I'd be here to help with the babies after work." And at night. And first thing in the morning.

"Then come on. We'll figure out details. Melly has her room set up already, and she seems happy here."

"Happy as a lark. She loves Sarah and is besotted by your babies." Not to mention her room here was bigger than the room they shared at his tiny apartment.

"And you? I mean, I need help, and I love your company, but I never want to take advantage."

Take advantage? This was a lovely mansion—a safe, wonderful home with a gourmet kitchen and plenty of room and a huge backyard for Melly to play in.

"If anyone would be taking advantage, it would be me. You know where I live, right? It would fit in your kitchen and dining room." He shook his head. They were both still dancing around this. He could take the bull by the horns. "I'd love to move in here."

"So we'll do it. We'll be a weird, wonderful unit."

"I love it. Thank you. Melly is going to be thrilled." And so was he. Totally and completely thrilled. It wasn't about getting to live in a fancy house, though. It was about who he got to live with. It was about the babies he'd been in love with since he first saw them. It was about having company, another adult. Logan.

"I'll draw up an agreement so you're protected, but I think we can do that Monday."

He trusted Logan, but the man was a lawyer, he would want—maybe even needed—to have everything wrapped up and outlined, signed, sealed, and delivered.

"Monday works for me. Melly and I could stay starting tonight—we were here for the weekend anyway—and then I'll move everything next weekend. There isn't a lot to bring." Most of his furniture wasn't worth keeping, certainly not worth moving into a nice, already furnished place like this. Hell, he'd seen the bedrooms here; they all had queen beds in them and that beat his little twin all to hell.

"Whatever you need, man. We'll work it out." Logan smiled at him. "You know how comforting it is, to know you'll be here?"

That warmed him through, and his smile back to Logan was both genuine and wide. "Then it's the right thing to do." He was so glad this wasn't one-sided, that he wasn't the only one who was getting something out of it.

Dirk looked to Sarah to see what she thought, surprised to find her gone, and Logan shrugged. "She's on her tablet, I'm sure."

He was glad he'd already spoken to her about it earlier. "She seems to be on board with me and Melly moving in. I'm glad." He couldn't have done it if it upset her.

"She's a good girl. She really is. I think she gets lonely too," Logan noted.

"We all do, eh? Does she have a lot of friends at Rebecca's?" He finished his last two bites of peanut butter and jam, and downed the rest of his milk. That had really hit the spot.

"She has friends at school, sure. She brings Cassie and Elena over a lot. You'll meet them. Funny little girls. They've been friends since pre-K."

"That's cool." He would be meeting Sarah's friends. So, he was really doing this. He was moving in with Logan and his daughter and his babies. It was going to be a whole new adventure. New and wonderful, he was sure.

He was going to.... Wow.

Chapter Five

LOGAN rocked little Seb and listened to Melly sing as she took her bath. There were ten children in his house. Ten. And only four of them were his. Rebecca had let him have Sarah again this weekend so she could participate in Dirk and Mel moving in.

Dirk was gone to move out of the scary little apartment with Dev and Aiden while Zack had stayed here to help him look after everyone's kids.

Ten children.

Wow.

Five was going to be a breeze when Zack, Aiden, and Dev took their kids and left. Sam and Suzy picked that exact moment to start wailing. Okay, maybe breeze was a bit strong of a word.

He put Seb down in his swing and picked up Sam, trying to put Suzy's pacifier back in.

"Holler if you need help," Zack told him, rocking with Dylan in his arms.

"Suzy is usually the patient one. She'll let me feed the boys first." Today she seemed less pleased to be pacified with the pacifier. He snorted at the thought. Pacified with the pacifier. How silly was that?

"Yeah? I wonder what that means for them growing up. Is she gonna have more patience than her brothers? Is she less hungry?" Zack shifted Dylan and cooed at the little boy.

"Or is she going to smother them in their sleep?" He chuckled and got Sam eating.

Zack laughed. "Well, her dad's a lawyer. I'm sure he'll be able to get her off." Zack rocked a little more, watching Logan feed his son. Then he asked, "So things are going well with Dirk and Melanie being here?"

"Yes. Is that weird or what? He just… it feels like he belongs. I… I don't know. He is here and I'm happy." Did it need to be more than that? And did he need to explain himself to his friends?

"Honey, we have a group of single dads called the Teddy Bear Club, and I'm holding the Baby Formerly Known as Unicorn. We passed weird a long time ago. And you're happy? That's what counts. Well, I guess that Dirk's happy too."

"I am. And I think he is too. That apartment wasn't a good place for Melly or her dad." Hell, he didn't think it was really a good place for anyone with kids.

"Yeah. It's less that it's small and more the area it's in. I'm glad you got them out of there, really. I think this whole situation is a win-win." Zack put Dylan on the floor, and he butt-scooted over to the blocks and his stepsister, Blaire. "Don't you whack him, Bee. I'm watching you."

She gave Zack an angelic look that Logan knew well hid a naughty nature. She wasn't mean, but she did like pushing. Logan managed not to laugh, but he had to turn away so she didn't see his smile.

"So… are you guys sharing a room?" Zack asked, clearly trying to sound super casual.

"We're… I don't know. No? I mean, we're not sleeping together, but we spend a lot of time in the same bed, sleeping." Logan wasn't sure that Dirk was interested in anything but the kids and the friendship, so he hadn't examined too closely if he wished it was more than that.

One of Zack's eyebrows went up, his friend staring at him.

"What? I just… I don't know."

"Okay." Zack paused a moment. "*That* is weird." Then he winked.

"I don't think he's into me, man."

Zack snorted. "You don't? Have you asked? Made a pass at him?"

"No. I don't remember how." He just looked for clues, and there weren't any.

Zack reached out and squeezed his shoulder. It looked like he had more to say, but the front door opened.

The guys all came in carrying boxes. Dirk came over, giving him a warm smile. "How's everything going here?"

Suzy immediately started screaming, kicking hard, demanding that Dirk pay attention to her. Then Melly and Lindsay ran through the room, wet and naked.

"My babies are crying!" Melly yelled as she ran through the room.

Dirk's mouth dropped open, but he put down his box and picked up Suzy. Then he laughed. "Streakers? Really?"

"Daddy! They're naked!" Sarah came in, looking like she couldn't figure out if she was tickled or horrified.

Dirk made a noise, and Logan could see he was trying desperately not to laugh. He gave up trying a moment later, sounds of mirth pouring from him. "I'll chase them down."

"You sit. I'll go." He put Sam down and went to find the naked toddlers. "Mel! Linds! Let's put our jammies on so we can have pizza and *Moana*!"

They beat him to Mel's room, and he got them settled there in her princess bed, watching the little TV with the promise of pizza when it came. There was nothing like Disney to fascinate. Which made life easier when there were ten kids in the house, three of them newborns.

Dirk met him outside the girls' room, coming from his room. "Hey. So that's it—I'm moved in."

"Welcome home. Seriously. I think Linds might be spending the night...."

"Eh, what's an extra kid or two?" Dirk laughed. "And thank you. It feels good to officially be out of that place. Although it's not quite real yet, you know?"

"...and this is my own room, and you can come visit my babies, and...."

Logan chuckled softly. "It is for Melly, huh?"

"Yeah, it sure is. And you'll have to keep an eye on the triplets—she's decided they're hers." Dirk leaned against the wall and smiled warmly at him.

"You noticed that. Are you happy to be here?" With me?

"I really am. Have I said thank you? Because thank you. I know that's not really adequate, but it's all I've got." Dirk stepped into his space and kissed the corner of his mouth, then hugged him tight. "Thank you."

He leaned for a second, soaking up Dirk's warmth, the solid, strong body. Dirk rested his head against Logan's shoulder, not seeming to be in a hurry to let go.

"Melly looks so happy. Like a princess in her bed with her friend." Dirk sighed. "This is perfect."

He didn't know what to say, so he just held on and enjoyed the feel of Dirk against him. They needed to go visit with the guys, pay for the pizza, check on the other little ones, but….

"You feel so good," Dirk whispered.

He blinked, then the fact that a portion of Dirk's body was stiffening against him sank in. Oh. Oh hell yes. He leaned, resting against that erect cock, feeling it. If Zack were to ask a certain question now, he'd have a different answer to it, wouldn't he?

"I… I'm sorry," Dirk said. Still, he didn't pull away.

"I'm not." Logan leaned in and brushed their lips together.

"Oh." The word was mostly sound, air sliding from Dirk's mouth to waft across Logan's lips. Then Dirk kissed him back, just as softly, their skin barely connecting. For all it was hardly a kiss, it warmed Logan through.

He couldn't quite believe this was happening to him. With Dirk.

One of the triplets started crying, which set off the other two, and Dirk rested their foreheads together, then gave him a quick peck. "Duty calls. Or should I say wails?"

"You need a piece of pizza anyway, hmm?"

Was this real? Really? How... magical. Dirk was so good with the babies, and now he was here, and he was sexy and seemed to be into Logan, and it was so much better than he had imagined having Dirk here would be. And he'd imagined it being darned good.

"Yeah, I could probably eat." They headed back downstairs to where the babies were. The wailing had stopped, which meant one of the guys was dealing with them. Which made it super tempting to duck into his room and explore a little more. They didn't, though. They were good and joined the others gathered in the living room.

Zack's twins and Sarah were in the media center watching *Coco*, and for the moment, each of the grown-ups could have a baby, hold it, rock it. He knew it was a short respite. Soon everyone would be gone and it would just be him and Dirk. Funny how not that long ago he wouldn't have been looking forward to that, but now he was. Not that he would have hated it, but it just would have been what it was. Now it was... something different.

"We'll start having meetings here," he suggested. Because then he wouldn't have to figure out how to get everything to the Roasty Bean.

Zack snorted at him. "Coffee's better at mine."

Dirk touched his back gently. "I bet once you're used to transporting them, being able to get out of the house for a while will be an important sanity break. And besides, Zack is right—the coffee is better at his."

"Traitor," he teased.

"Sorry, but I can't lie about stuff like coffee. There's a special place in hell for people who do that—a place where they don't have coffee."

"I like him," Zack pronounced.

So did Logan, but he only pretended to be offended for another moment before laughing.

Dirk gave a little bow. "Now, is the pizza here yet? Because I am starving, and I'd hate to have my stomach tear out of my torso and eat everyone."

"They said about forty-five minutes. Where are we on that?"

Zack looked at his watch. "Another fifteen minutes or so if they're on time."

"So we can relax for a bit." Dirk sat on the sofa and patted the spot next to him "Take a load off, Logan. I know those babies had you up most of the night."

"Suzy is not a sleeper. Not at all."

"I think she's the smartest of the bunch—she's learned that if she's awake when no one else is, she gets your full attention." Dirk's shoulder touched his briefly. "I'll have to remember that myself."

Aiden's eyebrow arched, and Logan did his best not to respond to his best friend's expression. "We'll have a lot of things to discover… together."

Dirk's warm smile was more than worth any looks Logan was getting from the others.

The front doorbell rang, and Logan levered himself up off the sofa, glad it had arrived early. "Pizza ahoy!"

"Saved by the bell," Aiden called out after him.

"You need any help?" Dirk asked.

"I got it." He'd ordered six pies—from fully loaded to cheese only and everything in between.

He gave the kid delivering them a nice tip, then carried the boxes into the living room and set them on the table. "Okay, everyone grab what you want. I promised Mel and Linds that I'd bring theirs up to them. Zack, can you bring Sarah a couple of pieces of pepperoni when you deliver whatever it is your girls want?"

"Of course. They want what Sarah wants, right?"

Dirk chuckled. "What if she wanted something they didn't like?"

"Oh, right now they would eat dirt if Sarah liked dirt. Those girls idolize her."

They all laughed, and Logan knew Mel was the same way. She was only in her room with *Moana* instead of in the living room with Sarah because she was tired and because she had Linds to share with.

"It would be cheaper to feed all of them dirt," Dirk noted.

"True, but I do love knowing that they'll all remember this—slumber parties and pizza and movies." In fact, this was what he wanted—kids and friends, a house filled with noise and laughter. This was what he'd always dreamed of.

"They will. They'll remember this amazing place full of people and good times." Dirk and Zack organized pizza for the crew in the media center while Logan gathered slices of cheese pizza onto plastic plates for Mel and Linds.

Both little girls were coloring and singing along with *Moana*. He set them up at the little table and chairs in the room. He was going to have to make sure that Mel didn't get used to food in the bedroom. He knew how quickly that could turn into a mess and bugs if dirty dishes got left in bedrooms.

By the time he got back to the living room, everyone was chowing down, concentrating on eating.

Dirk had one of the triplets over his thighs and another one on his shoulder as he noshed away on a piece of pizza. There was a space on the couch next to him, and Logan picked up Suzy from her bouncy chair and sat there, grabbing a slice of meatlovers. Dirk gave him a smile between bites.

"I do love a good greasy piece of pizza, don't you?" Dirk asked.

Was that a double entendre? Now that he knew Dirk wanted him, Logan was seeing them everywhere and trying to figure out why he hadn't noticed earlier.

Dirk grabbed a bottle. "Of course, it always tastes better if you have a cold beer with it."

"Moving deserves beer and pizza, right?" Dev grinned at Dirk.

"You know it. I think it might be a law or something." Dirk rubbed Sam's back with his free hand.

"This is a great place. I'm so glad you're making use of all this room, Logan." Aiden winked.

"So am I!" Dirk chimed in. "This place is so much nicer than where I was. Hell, I think I could put my whole apartment in this one room. Plus, you've got hot and cold running babies."

"And the kitchen. I love Logan's kitchen." Zack was rhapsodizing.

"That's because you cook," Dirk pointed out. Logan knew that Dirk wasn't hopeless in the kitchen, though everything the guy had made so far had been one-dish casseroles, cereal, or sandwiches.

Logan wasn't worthless. In fact, he did okay. He made one hell of a pancake. Between them, nobody starved.

The guys livened up once they'd all had a few slices, talking about the move, about their weeks like they hadn't just seen each other yesterday at the Roasty Bean. Logan let the conversation pour over him as he rocked and nibbled.

"So are we going to play a game of Monopoly or Risk or something?" Zack asked.

That reminded Logan of something he'd been pondering. "I think we should think about turning the basement into a huge game room. Playstation, pool table."

The entire room voiced their approval for that idea.

"We can all put in bits; it can be *our* playroom." Zack looked pleased as punch.

"An adult playroom. I like that. Although I guess we're all just big kids at heart." Dirk grabbed another slice. Four. Not that Logan was counting, but he did wonder where the guy put it all. The man was lean, fine.

He'd have to remember that. More than one steak for supper. Two burgers. Three, maybe four hot dogs. There had definitely not been any leftover chicken when they'd ordered it.

When Dirk finished, he got up and went to the kitchen. A few moments later, he came back out with three bottles and set them on the table, ready for the triplets.

"He's good," Dev said, and they all chuckled.

"They're on a schedule. Sam, Seb, Suzy." And it was working. He wasn't going to upset that apple cart for anything.

Dirk nodded. "And we're working hard to keep them on it. They're happier that way, and so are we."

Little Seb began to wiggle on Logan's shoulder, and he offered the sweet boy to his... Dirk. The exchange went smoothly, and Dirk popped the bottle in Seb's mouth. Seb latched on and began pulling at the milk. Zack reached for Sam, and that let Logan spend a little one-on-one time with his perfect baby girl.

The house was full, he had his babies and his daughter, and there was something interesting to explore with his new roommate. Things had really turned around in the last week. He hoped it just kept getting better.

Chapter Six

ONE of the good things about having friends with kids was that they got tired early too. All the girls had been settled, so they'd offered to have Zack's girls and Lindsay overnight. The triplets were settled too, and now it was just him and Logan awake. They were hunkered down under a blanket on the love seat in Logan's room, watching *Raiders of the Lost Ark*. It was the best way he could think of to end his first official day moved in.

"Are you happy? Glad to be home?" Logan hummed softly, the man so lovely in his sweats and his heavy socks. Which he knew sounded weird, but it was true. Maybe part of it was because Logan wasn't standing on ceremony for him, like he would with a guest. Logan was letting it all hang out.

"I am," Dirk told Logan. "Have I thanked you recently for letting me and Melly move in?"

"Once or twice. I love how she's just come home."

"Yeah, it's like she's been waiting for this place to happen. She's blossoming right before my eyes. It's more than just the place, though. It's her Unca Logan, the triplets." He and Melly were both really happy here, and it had far more to do with the other people who lived here than the furniture and whatnot.

"And Sarah," Logan added. "And I do love how Melly loves 'her babies.'"

"Yeah. I thought it would fade when she realized they don't actually *do* anything yet, but she still adores them more than anything. And yes, Sarah without question. She's always loved Sarah. I don't think she understands why Sarah isn't with us all the time, though," Dirk admitted.

"No? I miss her, but she's her mother's daughter, all the way."

"Yeah, I can see that. I just think Melly wants her to be here all the time. She's a great kid. She seems to be taking the invasion of not only babies, but me and Melly too, pretty well."

Logan smiled at him, then reached over and stroked his arm. The touch made him tingle. It made his skin stand up and take notice. He returned Logan's smile, knowing his was rather goofy.

"Hey," he said softly.

"I didn't know you were interested," Logan told him.

"No? I have been since we met. I guess I didn't know how to say so. I mean, you don't just come out and say it, do you? Maybe I should have."

"I think the way you did it was… perfect." Logan moved closer. "Kiss me, please?"

He smiled. Logan always knew exactly what to say. He met Logan halfway, pressing their lips together. The kiss was quiet, simple, and he had to moan. Oh. Oh, this was lovely. He let his eyes close as their lips continued to press together, moving slightly. How could anything so gentle and sweet make his balls ache so hard?

This was something he'd been praying for, for months.

He shifted a little closer and slid his hand along Logan's head until he was cupping the back of it. Then he touched his tongue to Logan's lips, wetting them. Logan leaned in, opening up and letting him in. He slid his tongue between Logan's lips, delving into Logan's mouth. Logan tasted a bit like pizza, but mostly like Logan. It was a good flavor.

Logan reached for him and wrapped one hand around his waist, the touch warm and heavy. He moaned into the kiss and shifted even closer, making it easier for them both to touch each other. With that in mind, he ran his free hand along the collar of Logan's shirt.

It felt so forbidden, so erotic, this little touch.

He'd been so good for weeks, and now he had free rein to explore, to learn Logan's body. They had a bunch of kids here; this wasn't going to be hot and heavy, but they could touch. Get to know each other.

For now he wanted to really appreciate each kiss, to feel how warm and wonderful each one made him feel. He was losing himself in it, moaning more and more, when the quiet night was broken by the wail of one of the triplets. Groaning, he rested their foreheads together.

"This is going to be our life, isn't it?" Logan chuckled hoarsely. "Let me grab her before she wakes the rest up."

"Yeah, for the next eighteen years or so." Dirk lay back, admiring Logan's ass until it was out of view. He didn't bother watching the movie—he just stared at nothing, enjoying the gently aroused feeling he had going.

He heard the baby hiccupping and whimpering, the sound easing. Suzy did love her alone time with Logan in the middle of the night. She was patient enough, but Dirk thought Suzy would be the one crawling into their bed in the middle of the night. That was okay, he already wore pajamas as he had Melly. She tended not to wake up needing comfort that often, but it was known to happen.

Logan came back to sit with him, the tiny baby on his shoulder. "Can we sit with you, Uncle Dirk?"

"Uh-huh." He leaned in and gave both daddy and baby a kiss on the cheek. She smelled so good. "Love that new baby smell."

"She's so funny—she's so standoffish when the boys are up, but like this? She's a cuddlebug."

"Would it be awful to suggest we take her to bed and cuddle her between us?" He wasn't sure what Suzy would think of that. She maybe wanted just her daddy.

"That would be good. She loves the attention, and I miss my bed."

"I can't think of anything I'd like better. Honestly." He got up and went to Logan's bed, tugged the covers down. He'd spent half the nights of his first week here, but they'd only slept. Not that they'd be doing anything but sleep this time, but now they both knew they wanted to, and that made it their bed instead of Logan's alone.

Funny how he hadn't even chosen a room to be his yet, and now he didn't need to.

Suzy fussed as Logan laid her down, but hushed as soon as Dirk reached for her.

"Little cuddlebug. I like that. Suits you to a T when you're away from your brothers, hmm?"

Her eyes were bright blue, focused on him like lasers. He wasn't sure she really could see clearly, but she heard him; she was paying attention. And she definitely knew who he was—could tell him apart from Logan. Dirk was convinced of that.

"You and your brothers are so wanted and so loved. You're a lucky little girl, aren't you? But you know who's even luckier? That's us—we got you and your brothers. So beautiful and adorable." He nattered on quietly.

"Three little girls and two little boys. Can you believe it?" Logan asked.

"No, not really. Yesterday I only had a little girl of my own. Now there's five little ones." The thought was wonderful and overwhelming, all at once.

Logan chuckled. "I know that look. I'm pretty sure I've been wearing it ever since I got the triplets."

"I know, right? It's like a miracle." He could agree with Logan on that. Except not only had he gained three babies and a wonderful little girl, but Logan as well. Okay, maybe he was making some assumptions, but Logan had asked him to move in, and there was something good happening between them he knew wasn't one-sided.

Logan nodded, one long hand on Suzy's belly. "It is. They are."

"Are you sure you don't mind that I've come in and appropriated your new family, your home, you?" Dirk asked. It felt like all his wishes were being granted, and he needed to make sure he wasn't making that happen at Logan's expense.

"I was lonely and overwhelmed. A little scared. I needed a friend, a partner."

"I'm glad to be here for you. For more than just the babies, eh?" He needed Logan to get that.

"And I'm glad you're here—for more than just the babies."

God, they were such dorks. He laughed softly at them both. Then he leaned in to give Logan a quick kiss. Logan returned it, at least until little Suzy slammed a tiny fist between them.

That had him laughing again. "She takes her daddy-and-me time very seriously."

"Indeed. Damn. She's a fighter."

"That's a good thing. Girls need to be able to stand up for themselves." He took her little hand and held it. So tiny.

She grabbed his finger and held on. Strong, too, for such a little thing. God, he loved her. That was the magic of babies. They made you fall in love just like that.

"She's keeping me," Dirk told Logan. "See?" He raised his finger slightly, her hand going up too. She definitely had a grip on him.

"Where's my phone? That's gorgeous." Logan snapped a picture and threw it on Instagram.

"These are going to be the most photographed babies ever." Dirk knew that probably wasn't true. All babies were superphotographed, especially now that it was so easy.

"We need to document their perfection."

"Absolutely." He wasn't going to argue with that.

Logan took a selfie with the three of them. "I love this."

He grinned, Logan's happiness infectious. "It's pretty special."

"I know, right? It's amazing."

Dirk had to admit he was happier than he'd ever been, aside from when Melly had been born. He let himself really feel it too. He would have to remember this when the kids were all screaming and unhappy and nothing would make them stop. Or when everyone was sick and miserable, including him, but he still had to cope. It was the moments like these that would tide him over the less than perfect times.

Chapter Seven

LOGAN sat in the middle of the floor surrounded by three screaming month-old babies and tried not to cry himself. Soon, he told himself. Soon Dirk would come home, and he could take a shower. Soon.

Seb's cries got louder, the sound piercing, and that had the others crying louder as well. Damn. Not soon enough.

Just as he was sure he was about to lose it, he heard the front door open. Thank the lord.

"Uh-huh. I bet Uncle Logan needs a hug," he heard.

Melly came running. "My babies are crying!" She sat next to Seb and patted his belly. "Don't cry, Sebbie. Melly is here."

"Damn, how long has this been going on?" Dirk asked, grabbing Suzy up and bouncing her on his shoulder. He put his free hand on Logan's shoulder and squeezed.

"A long time." Logan leaned back against Dirk's legs. "Hey, Melly."

"Hi, Unca Logan. Did you feed my babies?"

"Yes, honey, I've fed them."

"Did you change my babies' diapees?" she demanded.

"Yes, honey."

She pursed her lips, still patting Seb.

"You think they're sick?" Dirk asked as his bouncing hadn't quieted Suzy yet, though the frantic wails had backed off.

"No, I think they're evil demons." He managed a wink. One would doze off and another would scream, setting everyone off. It had been going on for hours.

"Well, I think Melly has Seb almost tamed. Did you try that white-noise-generator thingie?" Dirk asked.

He closed his eyes and counted to thirty. Of course he'd tried it. He wasn't an idiot. He was tired. He needed a shower. "Yeah."

"Damn. You look at your wit's end. Why don't you leave them to me and Melly and go for a walk or take a nap or something?"

"Okay. I need a shower. Now." A shower. A beer. A hard cry. "I'll be right back."

Dirk leaned in before he could go and gave him a quick kiss. "Take your time, eh?"

"Yeah. Thanks. Sorry." He took off, grabbing a beer before locking himself in the bathroom. He dialed Aiden, rocking on the closed toilet.

"Logan. Hey. What's up?"

"I suck. I totally suck at this."

"Ah, bad day, huh?" Aiden tsked. "We all have them, you know."

"Yeah. Yeah, what was I thinking?" He couldn't do this. He couldn't manage.

"You were thinking they'd give you an older kid, probably someone Sarah's age. And then they handed you three babies, and you fell in love with them." Aiden sounded so calm.

"Even Melly thinks I suck." He was going to cry. He sucked down a few gulps of beer.

"She does not—I've seen the two of you together. She thinks her Unca Logan hung the moon. You're just having a moment."

"I am. I'm locked in the bathroom drinking beer."

"Good for you. Take a shower when you're done. Hot water and soap can be magical."

"Tell me you don't hate me. Tell me the babies won't hate me." That was his biggest fear, failing everyone from the babies to his friends.

"Nobody hates you. Except maybe the people you go up against in the course of your job. Babies are hard, and we all have our moments."

He nodded, sniffling as he finished his beer. "I love you, man."

"I hope so—you're my best friend. And I don't hate you, I promise. I also promise that those babies don't hate you either."

"Okay. Okay, I believe you." He wasn't sure which was helping more: Aiden, the beer, or no longer being face-to-face with three inconsolable little bundles of what were supposed to be joy.

"Good. Shower, honey. Hot water. Maybe jack off."

He managed a half laugh for Aiden. Jack off. He could use that. He and Dirk had shared a bed for more than a week since Dirk had moved in and hadn't done more than kiss. If all the kids were asleep, they were too tired to do more than hold each other and kiss. If they weren't too tired—which was maybe for five minutes once a day—the kids were around. Honestly, Logan couldn't remember the last time he'd come.

He didn't know if he'd ever get it up again. Ever. He'd forget how to use it, and it would fall off.

He finished his beer and started the shower. Oh God, the hot water felt good. Amazing in fact. Logan let himself simply relax, let the water bash down on him and ease all his tension.

He was beginning to feel half human again when the door opened, Dirk peeking in. "Hey, Logan, how are you doing?"

"Hey. I'm sorry. I'll be right out."

"No, it's okay, take your time. They're asleep, and Melly's having a snack with Gru and the Minions. I just wanted to make sure you were okay."

"Yeah. Just a hard day. How was yours?"

"Okay. I gotta admit, I can't wait for school to be over. I keep thinking how I'd rather be home with you and the babies. It's like I've got a string attaching me to here, and the farther and longer I'm away, the tighter the string gets, trying to pull me back."

"Hell, you'd almost save money with Melly out of day care," Logan noted.

"Maybe. But then I wouldn't be contributing, and I'm already mooching off you."

"I'll have to pay a nanny. I can't do this alone." That much was clear to him. "I'm a bad father."

"Shut up—you're a great father!"

"I don't feel like one." He turned off the water and stepped out of the shower, blinking as Dirk gasped. "What?"

"You're beautiful."

It felt good having Dirk look at him like that.

"You are," Dirk insisted. "Beautiful. Hot. Sexy. All that water dripping off your gorgeous bod. You make me hungry."

Oh, how much had he needed to hear that? "Thank you."

"Maybe one day soon I can act on the desire to lick every drop off you."

"Wouldn't that be magical? I've forgotten what to do in that department." Though tired as he was, his cock was trying to say thank you for the compliments.

"I bet if we got twenty uninterrupted minutes alone when we weren't both exhausted we'd figure it out." Dirk leaned against the wall, watching him as he dried himself off. "So the other thing you mentioned. The nanny you need to pay who you haven't been able to find yet—if I wasn't working, I would be here full-time, and you wouldn't need a nanny. Then I would be contributing to the household, just not monetarily."

"I need help, Dirk. I don't know if I can do this without full-time help." He didn't want to make Dirk leave his job, but....

"Give me a try? You know how much I love the kids. You know I've just been putting in hours until summer holidays so I can be here full-time."

"Please." Logan felt such hope at the idea. Such relief. "Please, Dirk. I need you."

"I'll hand my resignation in tomorrow. I'll see if I can get away without giving them notice—there's plenty of subs who'd love to work full-time until the end of the term." Dirk reached for him. "Come on. You take a nap until supper, okay?"

"I'm okay. I really needed a shower." Dirk had been at work all day, and it wouldn't be fair to continue to abandon him with all the kids.

"But you can also have a nap." Dirk hugged him tight. "It's going to work out, Logan. You won't have to do it all alone all day anymore. Now go nap because I do have to get up tomorrow morning to hand in that resignation, so you're still on nighttime feeding duty."

"We ordering in?" Logan hadn't even thought about dinner yet, let alone prepped anything.

"Don't worry about supper. I'll take care of it." Dirk kissed him. "Go dream of me, eh?"

"Promise. Thank you. I just…. Thank you."

"No, thank you. I'm really happy about this. You, the kids, being here. All of it." Dirk gave him another hug, quick and hard, then slipped out of the bathroom.

Logan headed to the bed, and despite everything swimming around in his head, he swore he was asleep before he hit the pillow.

Chapter Eight

DIRK had handed in his resignation without notice. He knew he'd burned that bridge to the ground, but he'd seen the desperation in Logan's eyes. He knew Logan had been at his wit's end. And he couldn't stand the thought of some stranger helping out when it could be him.

This was what he wanted. He reminded himself of that many times in the first week of being home full-time, as they all found their way around each other and came up with a routine that let the kids all get what they needed and gave him and Logan most of what they needed too.

Tonight the triplets had gone down easier than they ever had, and he and Logan found themselves on the love seat in front of the television before 9:00

p.m. He wasn't exhausted. And he hoped Logan wasn't either. He really wanted to make love—finally. And he thought tonight was the night. But he wasn't sure how to initiate things now that it looked like they might be able to really get it on.

Logan turned to him suddenly and pulled him into a hard, intentional kiss.

Yes!

Moaning, he wrapped his arms around Logan's shoulders and kissed Logan back, his lips opening to let Logan in. Logan took his mouth like a starving man, leaning back and dragging Dirk over his long body.

Dirk moaned again, grabbing the base of Logan's T-shirt and hauling it up along his torso. Dirk made a soft noise when the T-shirt got stuck about halfway up Logan's body.

Logan helped and tore the offending shirt off. "Need you."

Dirk pulled his own T-shirt off, too, then lowered himself back down against Logan, moaning at being skin on skin. The heat of Logan's body was better than anything a cover or the fire could offer. "Me too. Like whoa." He ran his hands along Logan's sides.

"Uh-huh. Damn." Logan stretched up tall, offering himself.

Dirk pulled back enough to slide a hand between them and trace Logan's abs, then swept it up to feel the little points of Logan's nipples. He could hardly believe that he was finally getting to touch this beautiful man, to feel up the muscles he'd admired for months.

Logan hummed softly and twisted under his touch. Dirk rolled their bodies together, their cocks pressed tight with only some denim between them. Groaning, he slid his tongue into Logan's mouth. So many amazing sensations, he didn't know which to focus on.

With one hand pushed between them, Logan started working their jeans open. Dirk tried to keep his hips back so Logan had room, but he was out of his mind with the fact that they were doing this now, and his control was iffy at best.

"Can I touch you, babe?" Logan asked. "I want your cock."

"Please. Please." Dirk nodded. God yes. He needed this so badly. He couldn't even remember the last time he'd been touched. It had been ages since he'd even jacked himself off.

"Yeah." Logan tugged at his zipper, eased it down, careful of his sensitive parts.

He realized he was actually holding his breath as he waited for Logan to touch his cock, his entire body at attention. Logan kissed him, hard enough to make him gasp, and then warm fingers wrapped around his prick.

"Oh God. Yes, please." Dirk thrust his hips, sliding his cock along Logan's palm. He felt like shouting, like crying, like dancing.

"Feel good. Damn, honey." Logan's thumb brushed against the tip, sliding along Dirk's slit.

A shudder moved through him. "Oh God. Gonna come embarrassingly fast." He was almost there already from having Logan touch him. He hadn't been this easy to bring to orgasm since he'd first discovered it.

"It's been too long. I know. Here." Without warning, Logan shifted them, then swooped down and sucked him in in one long draw.

Dirk shoved his fist in his mouth to muffle his scream as he came down Logan's throat. Logan swallowed, taking him, making the pleasure go on and on.

He finally collapsed against the couch, panting. "Oh God, Logan. Thank you. Thank you."

"You're welcome. Damn, you taste good." Logan kissed the tip of his cock.

"You can taste me anytime you want." Like, anytime. He just hoped he had the opportunity to return the favor before they were interrupted.

"Thank you." The next kiss was soft, warm. Teasing.

He shivered. "Are you trying to keep me hard?" Because if Logan was, it was working.

"Don't you want to be hard? You can't make love to me if you're not hard."

"Oh damn." He nodded, his cock actually jerking at the thought. "Yes, please." He'd thought he was going to be sucking Logan off in return or something like that. Logan's idea was much better. Like, very much better.

"Well, then." He was taken back into that soft, hot mouth.

"Damn. Logan, that's... the best." Dirk thought Logan had to enjoy sucking, because he was so good at it. Funny, Logan seemed so.... Oh, why was he worrying? He was the luckiest man alive.

He dropped his hands to Logan's head and ran his fingers through Logan's hair, encouraging the suction and trying to let Logan know how good it was. Logan hummed and licked, loving on him, keeping him erect and needy.

"Thank you." He had to say it again, because while thank you wasn't enough, it was something. Soon he'd thank Logan as best he could. Thinking of that....

"What about you, Logan? What do you need?" He wasn't a selfish guy and he wouldn't keep making Logan pleasure him while Logan was getting nothing.

"I want you to make love to me," Logan reminded him. "Please."

"I'd love to." He brought their mouths together again, kissing Logan softly. "Come to bed. We'll get comfortable." He wasn't going to do something like this on the couch. They both deserved better.

Dirk got up and took Logan's hand to lead him over to his—their—bed.

Logan gripped his hand and went with him. "Oh, this is a lovely idea. I feel like I'm dreaming."

"Shh. Let's not wake up."

"Fair enough." Logan stripped down and stretched out on the comforter, giving Dirk the full naked view.

"Oh." Every now and then he saw Logan and his breath was stripped away. Literally. This was one such moment.

Hard and happy, Logan was ready for him, so lean and lovely. Dirk climbed onto the bed and knelt over Logan, sliding his hands along Logan's chest and belly and moving slowly to the pretty pink little nipples. Logan watched him like he was magical, like he was a god.

On the one hand, it made him feel special, important. On the other, there was a little voice in his head that told him he'd better perform at his best or else. Of course, he wanted to do nothing more than that, so it shouldn't be a problem.

"Kiss me? Please?" Logan begged.

Dirk brought their mouths together and slid their lips on each other. He could kiss this man forever.

He ran his hands over Logan's torso. He loved those muscles—he'd been admiring them for ages, and this was a luxury. Then he reached down, cupped Logan's heavy cock. Logan bucked for him and made a low, needy noise.

Dirk loved it, and he planned to do what he could to have Logan make a lot more of those noises.

"Need you, hmm?" Logan drew one leg drew up, exposing himself to Dirk.

"Oh yeah." Dirk nodded, fascinated by Logan's hole. He reached out, stroking it so carefully. Logan bucked again, and Dirk stroked it some more, loving the heat, the silkiness of the skin. "So hot."

"The lube is in the drawer, Dirk, and the condoms."

"Were you a Boy Scout? Because you're very well prepared." He kept stroking that little spot.

"I had hope. Someday. When the kids were grown and gone."

That made him giggle. "The condoms will be expired by then." Then he reached for Logan's lovely prick. He wrapped his hands around it, moaning at the heat and silkiness. Such softness around the hard core. "And it would be a shame to waste this lovely erection for that long."

"Oh. Oh, I concur. Absolutely."

He ran his hand along Logan's cock, then let it go so he could cup Logan's balls. They were heavy and hot and were the perfect weight in his palm. Logan spread even wider, a soft cry on the air.

"I've got you, I promise." He would have liked to have kissed Logan forever and spent just as long touching and learning every inch of Logan's body. Who knew how much time they had, though? Any of the kids could go off at any moment, and he wanted to make love to Logan before that happened.

He grabbed the lube and condoms out of the bedside-table drawer and then slicked up his fingers. Then he rubbed some more lube against Logan's hole. He loved the heat. He loved imagining himself sinking into it, Logan's body holding his cock tight. He moaned and pushed one of his fingers inside Logan's hole. Oh God, so tight.

"Yes." Logan arched and took him, demanding that he go deeper, farther.

Dirk obliged, pushing his finger all the way in and wriggling it around. Then he fucked Logan with it, watching Logan's face for a sign as to when to add a second finger. Once he was sure he'd seen the need ratcheting up, he slid his finger out and went right back in with two. Logan's body stretched to accommodate the added girth, and it made Dirk's balls ache a little. That was going to be his cock soon.

Logan moaned and rocked, riding his fingers with amazing need. "Dirk. Honey. Honey, please."

He shook his head. He knew they had to go fairly quickly, but he wasn't going to rush this. It had been a while since Logan had been made love to, and Dirk didn't want there to be any pain. So instead of pulling his fingers out and going in with his cock, he pushed a third finger into Logan's tight body. Logan gasped, that sweet body gripping him tightly, damn near milking him.

He groaned, resting his free hand on Logan's belly as he remained still, waiting for Logan to adjust to the added girth. He wanted it to happen already because it had been too long since he'd last done this too. At the same time, he was glad it had been. That made this time with Logan all the more special.

Bending, he set his lips against Logan's, breathing with him as much as kissing him. Logan moaned for him, over and over, that lean body still moving.

When the incredible grip eased around his fingers, Dirk began fucking Logan with them, pushing them deep. He managed not to cheer when Logan cried out and arched. He'd been hoping to find Logan's gland, and now that he had, he hit it again and again, making Logan writhe and dance for him.

He wasn't sure he was going to be able to wait much longer before he fucked Logan. His balls ached so bad, and he needed so hard. It had him panting.

Logan began to beg, soft little cries begging for his cock, for more, deeper, harder.

Dirk finally gave in to what they both wanted so badly and pulled his fingers out of Logan's body. His and Logan's groans of disappointment sounded together.

"Just need to glove up, L." He grabbed a condom and tore open the package with trembling fingers. He was so keyed up. So ready. He still wasn't steady as he worked the latex down over his cock, and he added more lube so he was super slick. Hopefully not too slick—so slick he couldn't actually get enough traction to push in. Oh God, he was losing his mind. He closed his eyes and took a deep breath. Okay. This was it. He just needed to focus on him and Logan and them being together.

"Hey. Hey, this is going to be good, honey," Logan told him. "I want you. You."

He kissed Logan. "Thank you." Then he lined up and pressed the head of his cock against Logan's entrance. They both moaned at the contact, and then he pushed, putting pressure on Logan's hole until it opened for him and the head of his cock popped into the wonderful tight heat.

"Dirk!"

The sound was loud, and Dirk trapped it in a kiss. Logan moaned, tongue fucking his lips.

Dirk worked his cock all the way in, then moaned and began to thrust, small movements for now as he let Logan get used to the feeling of his cock. He followed Logan's lead, though, driving in at the same speed as Logan's tongue assaulting his mouth. Fuck, it was the best thing ever. Ever. Logan was with him, right there, meeting every one of his thrusts, demanding his pleasure, their pleasure.

They found a rhythm that saw his cock come out a few inches before he pushed back in with force. He felt every inch of Logan's channel as it dragged along his cock, the sensations going straight to his balls. It was a damn good thing he'd already come or it would already be over.

Logan had a look of pure joy on his face, the expression blissful. Dirk could look at that forever.

He managed to get enough wits together to wrap a hand around Logan's cock. He stroked as he thrust, running his hand up and down along the hot, rigid flesh.

Logan bucked hard. "Oh. Oh damn. Please."

As he tugged on Logan's cock, each of his pulls was answered by Logan's body squeezing around him. He whimpered, the sensations almost overwhelming. God. God, he wasn't a virgin, but this felt big. Special.

"Logan." He whispered the name again and again, trying to be quiet, but he needed to let it out somehow. It was too much to contain silently.

"I have you. Please, love. Harder."

Grunting, he did as he was asked, pounding away at Logan now, his breath coming in short, needy pants. He lost all sense of everything except pushing into Logan's body, pulling at his cock, and the way it all felt too good to be true. But it was, and that blew his mind.

Logan accepted him, took him, begged for more.

Nothing this good could last, and he suddenly found himself barreling toward his orgasm. He squeezed Logan's cock tight, not wanting to go over the edge alone. "Together," he murmured. "Come with me." Like, soon. Like, now.

"Soon...." Oh, good man. Good man. "Now." Logan's ass clenched, bearing down on him.

"Yes!" He slammed in one more time, then froze as he came, spunk pouring out of him and filling the condom. He squeezed his hand rhythmically, wanting to make sure Logan came too.

Heat poured over his fingers, Logan sobbing softly.

"Sh...." The sound was automatic, and he giggled slightly afterward, a wave of happiness and ease washing over him.

"Uh-huh. Right. Sh."

"That's right. Sh." He rubbed their noses together, still smiling. He was sure it was goofy as hell, and he was sure he didn't care. "That was great. You're great."

"Uhn. You. That was.... Wow."

He beamed, loving that he'd rendered the man who made his living with words speechless. He kissed Logan, then grabbed the base of his cock, making sure he was holding on to the end of the condom as he pulled slowly out. He had to bite back his cry as he left that tight heat. He would have loved to stay in until he was soft.

Logan met his eyes. "Tell me we get to do this again."

"God, I hope so. And before they're eighteen too," he teased as he lay down next to Logan and cuddled up to him. They'd both need to put on pajama bottoms, but first he wanted to enjoy the feeling of Logan's skin against his. He'd always loved the cuddling afterward part of sex.

Logan's hand landed on his ass, drawing him in. "Thank you. That was perfect."

He nodded in total agreement. "Yeah. I think it's just what the doctor ordered. I'm even looking forward to middle of the night feedings now." And that was saying something.

"You are a sick man." Logan tickled his ribs, playing with him.

He laughed, squirming against Logan as he tried in vain to get away from Logan's fingers. He bit his bottom lip in an attempt to not be too loud. He felt closer to Logan now—not just physically, but emotionally too. They'd connected on a deeper level.

Logan hugged him, held him tight. "Oh, this has been the best day."

"I'll second that. Hell, I'll third and fourth and fifth it." He nibbled on Logan's earlobe. He felt boneless, sexy in a lazy, easy way, and he wasn't ready to fall asleep yet. He wanted to keep feeling like this.

Logan grinned at him. "It's amazing what an orgasm can do for you."

"Uh-huh. And I got two. We're not keeping score, though, eh?" Because he wasn't sure that first one had really counted, considering how quick he'd been off the mark. Embarrassingly so, really.

"No. No, I did love sucking you. I may have to make it a habit."

His cock tried to make a comeback, jerking against Logan's leg. "I could get behind that becoming a habit." Behind, beside, in front of. He was happy to have it on offer.

"You're something." Logan kissed him, a gentle touch of their lips together. "Thank you, honey, for being here."

"Thank you for having me. There's nowhere I'd rather be." As busy as it was here, twenty-four seven, he was where he was supposed to be, and he was loving it. Even when the babies were screaming in unison.

Logan kissed his knuckles, and they pulled the covers up. They could put on pants at the 2:00 a.m. feeding.

He brought their lips together, his eyes closed as he concentrated on the easy kisses. He knew he would remember this moment forever.

Chapter Nine

LOGAN sat with Melly, reading to her, rocking her. He found himself enchanted with her, how fierce and smart she was, how adaptable. Dirk had done an amazing job raising her. It boded well for the triplets, not only to have a proven dad like Dirk helping to bring them up, but two big sisters to lead the way for them, teach them how to be independent and strong.

"Unca Logan?"

"Yeah, Melly?"

"Can we have a swing set in the backyard?"

He grinned. That didn't sound like a terrible idea. "You think we need one?"

"Uh-huh. With baby swings and a slide and a swing for daddies and uncas."

"And maybe a playhouse?" He knew Sarah still used her playhouse at her mom's.

"A playhouse with a kitchen!" She clapped her hands, her eyes shining at him. "With a picnic bench, and we can have tea parties in it, and I can be the daddy, and Sarah can be the mommy."

"Whatever you want, baby. We should talk to your daddy, see what he thinks."

"Da will agree with me. He knows I look after the babies." Melly was very committed to making sure the triplets had everything she thought they needed.

"He will agree with you, will he?" He thought she sounded so grown-up.

She nodded quite seriously, curled up happily against him. "He agrees with me except for ice cream."

"Oh? What about ice cream?"

"We can't have it for supper." She pouted. So utterly adorable he wanted to run and get her ice cream right now.

"No? Supper tends to need vegetables and things, doesn't it?"

"Who made that rule?" she asked. "Because I don't think it's a very good rule."

"I think it was grandmas." He threw them right under the bus, just like that.

Melly's little brow wrinkled, along with her nose. "But grandmas have candy," she pronounced, as if vegetables and candy were mutually exclusive.

His phone rang, and he grabbed it. The phone number was unfamiliar but local, so he answered. "Hello?"

"Hello, Mr. Bartram, this is Detective McMann. Are you at home, sir?"

"Pardon me? Detective who? What is this about?" Why hadn't they called the firm? Or if they had, why had the firm given out his home number? He was going to have words with someone.

"I need to speak to you, sir, immediately. Are you home?"

Logan frowned. "Yes. Yes, I am. What is going on?"

"We'll be there in five minutes, sir."

The phone went dead, and he smiled at Melly. "Honey, I have someone coming to see me. Let's find Daddy."

"He's sleeping with the babies," she reminded him, standing and taking his hand. When they were super fussy, nothing settled the triplets faster than Dirk rocking with them.

Logan and Melly went to the nursery to find Dirk rocking with Seb, the other two in their swings, fast asleep. Dirk and Seb were both awake, having an intense-looking conversation. No doubt solving the problems of the world.

"Hey, I need you to keep Melly in here helping with the babies. I have an important person coming to see me."

Dirk sat up, hand cradling Seb's head. "What's up?"

"C-o-p-s," he spelled.

"I thought you weren't working until the kids were older?" Dirk waited for Melly to sit, then gave her Seb, staying close enough to keep Seb from falling if necessary.

"I'm not." *Pay attention, goddamn it. This is serious.*

Dirk frowned, looking like Melly for a moment. "Okay…. Go on. Melly and I have the babies."

"Thanks, babe. I'll be back." He wasn't sure what the fuck was up, but the cops coming to your door was never, ever good. He tried to imagine what client he had that could be dangerous, but he wasn't a criminal lawyer. He did real estate and family litigation.

The knock was sure, solid. He opened the door to find two officers with their hats in their hands.

"Can I help you?"

"I'm sorry, sir. You are named as Rebecca Wentworth's next of kin?"

He nodded, and the next few moments were snippets of words—car accident, massive head trauma, passed away—but the only thing he wanted to know was "Our daughter. Was our daughter in the car?"

"No, sir. She was still at school when the accident happened. She's currently at the day care at the hospital."

"Does she know?" He searched for his car keys, keeping his focus on Sarah. "Have they told her anything?" God, his baby. Come on. Keys. Where the fuck were his keys?

"I don't know what she's been told. Is there anyone else at home, sir? Maybe someone who could drive you?"

"No. No, I mean, yes. My partner is home, but he's with our other children. I...." His knees tried to buckle, but he couldn't let them. "I have to get to my daughter. Now."

"Is there someone you can call? I don't think you should be driving at the moment." The officer didn't look like he was going to let Logan out of the house.

"Just a minute. Can you please drive me to my daughter and I'll have a friend pick us up?"

"We can do that. Are you ready to go?"

"Let me tell my partner. Two seconds." He ran back to the nursery. "I need to speak to you, Dirk. Please."

Dirk said something to Melly, then came over and gave him a tight hug. "You look green—what's wrong?"

"I— Rebecca."

Dirk clutched him tighter. "Oh my God, is Sarah okay?" he whispered.

"Rebecca was killed in an accident. I have to get Sarah. Call someone and have them call me and come get me at the hospital."

"Oh my God," Dirk said again. "Oh my God. Okay. Okay. You're taking a cab or something to get her?" Dirk gripped his shoulders and squeezed.

"The police will take me. You try and warn Mel. I don't know what Sarah knows. I'll be back." He turned and headed back out at a run. "Please. I need my daughter."

"Don't worry about anything here," Dirk called after him. "I've got it. You get Sarah. Love you."

"Love you. Call Aiden!"

"I will. Hug her for me!"

The two officers were patiently waiting for him when he got back downstairs, talking quietly to each other. They looked up when he got there and gave him nods.

"I need to see my daughter." He needed his baby in his arms. It was all he could think about right now. Thank God for Dirk so he could just think of Sarah.

"We're ready to drive you to the hospital." One of the men opened his front door for him, and he followed the other out to the squad car in front of his house.

A part of him couldn't believe this was real, but the rest of him was all too aware that it was.

He wasn't going to start crying. Not yet. He was going to get his little girl and bring her home. Nothing else was important. Nothing else in all the world.

Chapter Ten

DIRK looked out the window again, hoping to see Aiden's van heralding the return of Logan with Sarah. Still nothing. He paced to the front hall and checked out the side window. Then he made himself go to the kitchen to put on another pot of coffee.

He skirted Dev and Zack, who were sitting around the coffee table, talking quietly together. In the kitchen he found a variety of sweets and casseroles on the counter.

It was a morbid repeat of the day they'd brought the triplets home. Only he wasn't with Logan, and his lover needed him really badly right now. Of course, Logan had also needed him to look after the kids here, so here he was.

Thank goodness everyone had shown up after he'd called Aiden. He was all keyed up and tense, and the triplets could feel that and had been cranky ever since Logan had shared the news. He really needed Logan to get back. He needed to be there with him.

"Aiden is on his way with them. Sarah had to be sedated because she kept vomiting, so it took a while." Dev sighed. "God, this sucks. This sucks so bad. Poor little girl."

"Oh God." He ran his hand through his hair, feeling so helpless. He'd lost Melly's mom at childbirth, so while she had no mom either, Melly didn't remember her. It wasn't the same thing at all. He gave Dev a hug. "Thanks for letting me know. I was beginning to worry." Beginning to. He snorted.

"Do you want us to stay for a few days? Help out? We totally will," Dev offered.

God, they had the most wonderful friends in the world.

"I don't know. I don't know what Logan's going to want. Or what Sarah will need. Can we play it by ear?"

"Of course. I don't know if he's going to want to stay with her at Rebecca's. If so you'll need help with the wee ones. You tell us. We love you."

"You guys are the best. Really." He took another hug from Dev. "Thank you." He honestly didn't know how he'd have survived the wait without them.

"That's what friends are for. They're here."

He nodded jerkily and gave Dev a last squeeze. He all but ran to the front hall and opened the door for them. He peered out.

Logan opened the van door and lifted Sarah out, the ten-year-old looking like nothing but a tired little girl. Poor sweet thing. He couldn't imagine anything worse happening to her. Melly came to his side and held on to his hand. He squeezed gently. They would do everything they could to help Logan and Sarah with this. He knew Melly would do anything for her beloved Sarah.

"Daddy? What's wrong?"

He went down on his haunches and looked her in the eyes. "You know how your mommy went to heaven when you were just born? Well, Sarah's mommy just went to heaven, and Sarah is really sad."

"Oh. Oh, I will hug her."

Logan shook his head as he came in, tears streaking his cheeks, and headed upstairs to the wonderful little garret that was Sarah's room. They were going to have to go get her things, her schoolbooks, everything.

What about the house? What about…. God. He went to follow Logan up, see what he could do, and he realized that Melly was ahead of him, eager to comfort her new big sister.

"Sarah. I will sleep with you so you're not lonely. I promise. I will be right with you."

"Honey, Sarah's—" Logan started, but Sarah shook her head.

"It's okay. She can stay. She's just a little girl. She doesn't understand." Soft sobs started, and Logan sat on the bed, holding her, rocking her.

Melly climbed up and cuddled on the other side of Sarah. She patted Sarah's hand. "I understand having a mom in heaven."

Sarah collapsed, and the soft wails broke Dirk's heart.

"Babe, can you get Sarah a glass of Sprite please? Maybe a piece of toast for later?" Logan asked.

"We've got saltines. I'll bring up some of those." His mom had always had those on hand for when he was sick. It still made him feel better when he was under the weather. "You need anything else?"

"I'd take a drink, please." Logan carefully took Sarah's shoes off.

"You got it." He would bring Logan a bottle of water as well as a snifter of brandy. He had a feeling Logan needed the shot, even if he didn't realize he did. He'd worry about getting food into Logan after Sarah was asleep.

He went back downstairs, feeling like he wasn't doing enough but knowing Logan needed him to do the things he was doing.

Aiden was holding little Dylan, hugging him. "Hey, honey. How are they?"

He shook his head. They weren't great. He imagined they wouldn't be great for some time. Especially Sarah. "I'm getting some food and drinks for them."

"I've talked to Zack and Dev. Zack will take the twins and my oldest to his place. Dev will stay here with the little ones while I take care of some things. Then we'll both help out for a couple of days with the babies, okay?"

"Yeah? That really rocks, guys." In fact it made him mist up a little. He blinked rapidly a few times. "Thank you."

"Yeah, he'll bring Lindsay back tomorrow. She and Melly can play."

"Sounds good. Seriously, thanks everyone." He hugged Zack and Aiden, then left them to sort themselves out as he went to the kitchen to put together a tray of food to tempt a very sad little girl with an upset tummy, and her daddy, as well as the drinks he'd promised.

"Da! Da, Sarah threw up. Unca Logan said to help you while he helps her clean up and get in jammies."

He picked Melly up as she came running in and wrapped her in a tight hug. He had her. He did. "I love you, Melly. Sooo much."

Her little arms wrapped around his neck, and she squeezed. "Love you, Da." She smacked a kiss on his cheek.

God. God, what was he going to do? Five kids, three infants, a little girl who'd just lost her mother.... He didn't know if it made it worse or better that he'd only met Rebecca a few times, so he didn't know her that well. His mourning was more for Logan and Sarah than anything else.

"No one would blame you if you ran screaming," Zack said, coming into the kitchen and kissing Dirk's cheek. "I'm heading out. Would you like me to take Mel?"

"Thanks, but no. She wants to be there for Sarah, and I think that would be good for both of them." He thought it would make it harder on Melly if she were taken away from them, no matter how well-meant.

"Okay. She's a good sister." Zack smiled at Melly, and she nodded.

"I will hold her and make it better."

And Dirk believed that truly would help. He gave his daughter a warm smile and put a tray down on the table. "You want to put some crackers on that and maybe some grapes, sweetie?"

"Yes, Da. I will help."

Zack hugged him. "Okay, you have my number, you have the guys, and you have all the help we can muster."

"Thank you. Thank you." He watched Zack go, then went back to pouring out drinks and helping Melly arrange the food. At the last minute, he added a bottle of Children's Tylenol. "Okay, that looks like a good tray to tempt sad people, doesn't it?"

"There's something missing, Da."

"What's that?"

"Ice cream."

Oh, that was super adorable. Even if ice cream would be too heavy on Sarah's upset tummy. "How about a Popsicle instead?" Cold and sugary, but also pretty much all water, it was more likely to stay down.

"Okay, Da. An orange one."

"Fine. Grab it for me, and let's go."

He carried the tray while Melly carried the Popsicle, and they went all the way up to Sarah's room.

"Quiet, just in case they're asleep," he murmured when they got to the half-open door.

Logan was holding Sarah, who was sleeping in his arms. As soon as the door opened, she tried to wake up, open her eyes. "My head hurts."

"I've brought some kiddie Tylenol, and there's lots of water, among other things." He set the tray down at the foot of the bed and passed the bottle of pills and a glass of water to Logan. "And Melly brought you an orange Popsicle."

"Thank you." Sarah looked shaky. "Daddy says I can come live here. Right now."

"Of course you can, honey. This is your house too. You even have your own bedroom here. This is your home."

"See? I told you. This is your home. Always."

Melly climbed up on the bed to sit next to Sarah, took the wrapper off the Popsicle, and handed it over. "Orange is the best flavor."

"Thanks, Melly." Sarah's eyes were huge and swollen, and Dirk went to fetch a cold rag. *Poor baby.*

He suspected he would have that thought on repeat for a while to come.

When he came back, Sarah was sucking on the Popsicle while Melly ran a brush through her hair, gently, over and over.

He was so proud of his girl. She was so caring, so nurturing. He knew that would help Sarah get through this. He just wished there was nothing to be getting through.

He handed Logan the cold washcloth and let him fold it and put it across Sarah's eyes. She sighed and leaned against her daddy, her breath hiccupping now and then. Every time it did, Melly patted her arm.

Dirk felt so fucking helpless. "Can I do anything for you, Logan?" Anything at all.

"Are the babies sleeping?"

"They are, and Dev is still here, helping out. Aiden's going to come as well. He's getting Linds to Zack's for a sleepover and picking up a few things for them and Dylan. They've got our backs." Speaking of backs, he put his hands on Logan's shoulders and began to massage. Poor man was tight as a board.

Logan leaned into him, and he handed over the liquor. "You need it."

It looked like Logan might protest, and he massaged harder.

"You need it, and there are three other adults here to look after the triplets. They aren't going to remember you weren't with them tonight when they're grown. Hell, they're not going to remember tomorrow. So take care of yourself and Sarah, hmm? Drink." He kept massaging, moving from close to Logan's neck all the way out along his shoulders to the round of them. He ran his hands up and down along Logan's arms, then returned to working the tight muscles across Logan's back.

Logan shot back his drink, throat working. "Thanks, honey. This is… unexpected."

Dirk leaned in and hugged Logan from behind, careful not to dislodge Sarah. "It's a tragedy, and you never expect those. My heart is breaking for you both. But we'll get through it together. All of us, and our friends. We're a strong family."

"I want to go home, Daddy. Please. Make them bring her back." The broken tones of Sarah's pleas broke Dirk's heart all over again.

"Sh. Just rest. Please, baby."

"Do you want to sleep with Melly in her bed tonight?" Dirk asked. "Or she could sleep up here with you."

Sarah turned her swollen eyes on Logan. "Can I sleep downstairs, Daddy? Please?"

"Of course. Anything you want."

"I want Mommy back!" Her face crumpled, and she started crying again, horrible, jagged sobs that were so hard to hear. He wished he could take this for her.

Melly's face twisted up, a few tears leaking. It was impossible not to be moved in the wake of Sarah's grief.

"I do too, baby. I'm so sorry." Tears slid down Logan's cheeks.

Dirk held on and rocked Logan, knowing that, for the moment, this was the best he could do. Healing would come, but right now they all needed to hold each other.

Chapter Eleven

SARAH and Melly lay together in Melly's bed, and once they were finally asleep, Logan and Dirk headed downstairs. Aiden and Dev were sitting in the kitchen, drinking coffee.

Aiden came right to Logan and held him close, and his legs buckled, his sobs rocking him. Aiden had known Rebecca all along; Logan had discussed having Sarah with him. Aiden knew what a wonderful woman she was. Had been.

Dirk hovered, looking like he didn't know what to do.

"Come on. Come on, man." Aiden got Logan to a chair, sat him down. "Breathe."

Right. Breathe. He could do that, right?

"You want something to eat?" Dirk asked. "We have a bunch of stuff people brought."

"No. A roll maybe? Something small? It was just an accident. No one was drunk. No one was speeding. This man had a heart attack and died behind the wheel."

"That really sucks," Dirk noted as he fussed around, finding a plate and something for Logan to eat.

"Shit happens." Aiden sat close, took Logan's hand. "You never know when your number is up, and as often as not you don't get a warning. And it sucks for those left behind. We're all here for you guys, though. You're going to hear that a lot over the next few months, but that's because it's important to remember."

Suzy started wailing, and Logan made to jump to his feet, but Aiden put a hand on his back and encouraged him to stay put while Dev got up. "We'll take over baby duty tonight. You take some time to grieve and to sleep."

"And you need food and to focus on Sarah. She'll have a rough few days." Aiden squeezed his hand.

Dirk put a roast beef sandwich and a glass of milk in front of him. The sandwich had a tiny bit of mayo and a tiny bit of ketchup, just how he liked it. Dirk knew him well.

"Thanks, honey. I'm just... it doesn't seem real, not at all." And yet it hurt like a mofo anyway.

"I know." Dirk sat next to him. "I can't really believe it."

"They say she never felt anything." That meant something, right? Everyone kept saying it like it did.

"That's good. I bet she never even saw it coming. No pain, no fear." Dirk put the sandwich in his hand.

"That's right. I need to find her will, her information. I know she had great life insurance; so do I." He had copies of all her papers here and at the office.

Dirk stood and wandered around the kitchen. "Sarah will be set, hmm? You won't have to worry about providing for her, sending her to college."

"You don't have to worry about any of that right now," Aiden told him. "Eat, have a shot of something hard, and get some sleep. That's what you need right now."

Dev nodded. "Tomorrow we'll start with funeral arrangements."

"Oh God. How am I supposed to make Sarah sit through her mother's funeral?"

"It's not going to be easy, but it'll help her." Dirk wiped down the counters. "In the long run, I mean."

"Or if she doesn't want to, don't make her." Dev sounded sure. "Did Rebecca want a service?"

"I have no idea." He rubbed his face. He had no idea about anything, except that this sucked and he wanted her back, just like Sarah did.

"You want me and Dev or Aiden to go to her place and find the important papers?" Dirk asked. "So you don't have to go back there?"

"I have her will and her insurance papers. We'll start there. I'm her executor." He would have to deal. It was his job.

"Okay." Dirk came to stand behind him again, squeezing his shoulders. "But tomorrow. It's not going anywhere."

"Right. Tomorrow. Today we just remember her and take care of Sarah."

"And you." Dirk kissed the top of his head.

"You do a good job of that." He leaned into Dirk's body. This would have been even harder without Dirk.

"That's because I love you, and your health and happiness are important to me." Dirk was solid and warm, hands just right against his collarbones.

"I hope you're ready to have another child full-time," Aiden said.

Dirk answered before he could. "We'll always have room for Sarah in our lives and in our hearts, full-time."

"Of course. She's my first baby girl." He didn't want it to happen like this, though.

"And she knows you, knows this place. She'll be able to heal here."

He looked into Dirk's eyes. "Promise?"

Dirk cupped his cheeks, looked right back at him. "I promise. You and your beautiful girl are going to make it through this. You're both going to heal."

Logan began to cry again, and he reached for Dirk. His lover pressed in close and held him tight. Then Dirk started to rock him, hand sliding along his back. "Come to bed, Logan. You need to rest. You're going to make yourself sick."

He shook his head, but Dirk stood and took his hands, tugging him up. "Bed. I'll hold you all night long."

"We've got the babies. Just relax and rest." Dev nodded.

He let Dirk pull him to his feet. One arm around his waist, Dirk supported him as they made their way to the staircase and headed up to the bedroom.

"I love you." Logan was leaning more than he'd meant to, but Dirk seemed to have him. "I'm so…. Thank God you're here."

"I love you too, and I've got your back." They passed the triplets' room, and he heard Dev murmuring to the babies. None of them were crying. Okay. They were okay. They checked in on the girls too. Melly and Sarah lay curled up together, both still asleep, thank God.

Then Dirk led him to his bedroom and over to the bed.

"Let's get your clothes off and your pajamas on."

"I feel... disconnected." Like he was in a different reality. God, he wished that was true.

"I'm not surprised." Dirk took Logan's shirt off him, then undid his belt and pulled it off through the loops. "You want to talk about it?"

"I need you to tell me Sarah is going to be okay." That was the important part.

Dirk cupped his face again and gazed into his eyes. "Sarah is going to be okay."

"I'm going to believe you."

"You'd better. Or else." Dirk tugged his slacks down, then helped him into his pajama bottoms.

Logan stared at nothing, letting Dirk help him. As soon as Dirk had him in his pajamas, he helped Logan climb into bed.

"Hold me. Just for a minute." Logan needed that.

"No way! I am going to hold you all night long." Dirk stripped quickly, climbed into bed with him, and wrapped him up in warm, solid arms. All he had to do was cuddle in.

Dirk gently stroked his back and murmured soft incomprehensible words that sounded like comfort and love.

"I'm sorry about all this, love. You've had so much change." What if it got to be too much for Dirk?

"You don't have anything to apologize for. And you've had just as much change. Only this is far worse than anything I've gone through. Don't worry about me; focus on your daughter. I love you so much."

Logan held on tight. "I love you. Thank you."

"Anything. Anytime. Anywhere."

Logan hoped that remained true when things got rough with Sarah and the babies teething and all. He would need Dirk more than ever.

"Sh... stop thinking. Rest. Please."

One of the babies cried out, and he tensed, getting ready to go. Dirk held him tighter.

"There are other grown-ups here ready to deal with babies. Rest. Sleep."

Sure enough the baby quieted, taken care of.

"She never felt it. She didn't hurt." It turned out that was indeed a huge comfort. No pain.

"That's good. That's how we all want to go, right? No warning, no pain, just boom. It's too bad it was so young."

"Yes. Yes, exactly." He sighed, shook his head. "At least Sarah wasn't in the car."

"Yeah." Dirk squeezed him extra tight. "She's safe. And she's going to be okay. I'm not saying it'll be easy, but she's going to get through it." Dirk kissed his shoulder, lips soft and warm, gentle. "Now, please, you need to get some sleep. It'll help, I promise."

"Right. Right." He closed his eyes, his head throbbing. It would get better. Dirk had promised. He knew in the back of his head that Dirk couldn't actually promise that, but he shut that part of his brain off. He wanted to believe Dirk's promise.

Dirk hummed softly. Logan thought it was one of the lullabies they sang to the triplets, but he couldn't be sure. It didn't matter. The sound was soothing, and it was surprisingly easy to push everything else behind it and let it take him away.

Chapter Twelve

DIRK checked in on Logan and the babies. They were all asleep, Logan looking even more exhausted than Dirk felt. He checked on Melly next, finding her curled up in the middle of her bed with her dollies and animals tucked in all around her.

That just left Sarah. The funeral had been disastrous, and she'd run upstairs to her room. That had been four days ago, and she hadn't come down at all. Only Logan had been allowed in her room, and even that had been under protest. Dirk knew Logan had brought her food, but he wasn't sure she'd actually eaten anything.

So he made a peanut butter and jam sandwich and grabbed a couple of cookies and a small bowl of strawberry ice cream, along with a glass of milk. Putting it all on a tray, he headed up to Sarah's bedroom.

Maybe she'd talk to him, maybe she'd eat. Maybe she'd scream at him and throw him out, but he was going to try to get through to her.

He knocked gently on her door so she knew he was there, but he didn't wait for an answer—he let himself in.

The smell of stress and sweat was awful, the look of loss and agony on Sarah's face worse.

He needed to get her into a bath or a shower, open the windows, and change her sheets. Nobody could heal in an environment like this.

"Hey, honey. How about I draw you a bath? You can sit in there in the dark if you like. Or bring your Bluetooth speaker and listen to some music?" He wouldn't make her talk to him or listen to him or, really, interact in any significant way with him, but he would care for her.

She sniffled. "My head hurts. Bad."

Yeah, he imagined it did. No eating, all that crying. She had to be as miserable physically as she felt emotionally. "There's Tylenol in the bathroom. Come with me?" He set the tray on the bedside table. She could eat when she got back. He'd just take away the ice cream and get some juice to add to the tray once she was in the tub.

"Is that ice cream? Melly left some?"

"She did. She said that strawberry was your favorite flavor. It would taste delicious with a strawberry bubble bath to sit in, wouldn't it?"

"Can I eat it in the bathtub?" She looked at him, and he could see she was asking to come back to life.

"I think that's a great idea. Why don't you grab the bowl and follow me." He went to the little en suite Logan had built up here for her, trusting she was following, and started the bath, pouring some bubble bath in as the water started filling the tub.

Sarah ate a bite while she waited. "It's good."

"Yeah? My favorite is vanilla, although I had a toasted coconut once that was absolutely amazing." Once the bath had run, he grabbed a Tylenol and poured a glass of water, setting them on the edge of the tub. "I'll leave you to it, but if you need anything, just call, okay?"

"Okay. Thank you." That was a smile. Okay. Okay, then.

He went back to the bedroom and got to work—opening windows and emptying trash, changing sheets. The room smelled better just for getting the windows open. No one needed to live like this. She wasn't dead. She needed to go back to school, remember that she had a life.

Dirk thought he was going to have to be the one to make her do it too. Logan was feeling too close to it himself, and he was in charge of dealing with Rebecca's things—the house and all its furnishings, the insurance, the business, everything.

Once he had the room picked up and the sheets and Sarah's dirty clothes moved to the laundry room, he went and got her some juice. He thought maybe she'd be happier with that than the milk. If he had a headache, that was the kind of drink he preferred. Then he returned to the bathroom and knocked on the door.

"How are you doing?" he asked.

"Okay." She opened the door, trying to dry her soaking hair. "Can you help me?"

"Sure thing." He grabbed another towel and began drying her hair like he would Melly's. Sarah's was longer, but the principle was the same. "How's your headache?"

"Better. Thank you."

"That's great." He got most of the water out of her hair. "Do you want me to brush it out for you?" He enjoyed doing Melly's, and it was a great time for some daddy-daughter conversation.

"Do you pull?"

"I try very hard not to. I do have experience. I do it for Melly."

"Okay. Okay. I'm just…. It's long."

"It is. I'll sit on the chair and you can sit on the ottoman in front of me. Oh, I need your brush."

"I'll get it." She disappeared into the bathroom and came out with a brush. Sweet baby. She looked like she could pack a week's worth of clothes in the bags under her eyes.

"That's a pretty nightie," he noted as he sat down, making easy conversation.

"Thank you. Daddy gave it to me for Christmas. Do you know what's going to happen to all my other ones?"

"Your daddy is taking care of everything at your other house. He'll pack up your stuff and bring it here." He started brushing her hair, very carefully working out the tangles so he wouldn't pull.

"All of it?"

"All of it."

"Okay." She sighed, then let her head fall forward.

Had she been up here worrying about that for the last four days? He shook his head but didn't press her on it. He kept brushing her hair.

After a while he noted casually, "Are you ready to go back to school on Monday?"

"Already?"

"We have your schoolbag here. I could drive you. What do you think about that?"

"Everyone will know, Dirk. Everyone."

"Yeah, they will. But that's going to be true if you go back tomorrow or the day after that or next week or next month." He'd gotten all the tangles out, but he was hoping the brushing motions were soothing, so he kept going. "I seem to remember you saying how much you liked school." And she was doing really well too. Logan had been bragging on her right before this had happened.

"What if I cry? Everyone will make fun of me."

"Not everyone. What about your best friends? They were at the service."

"Cassie and Elena? They're good. Cool."

"So they're not going to make fun of you. And if you think you're going to cry, I bet if you tell your teacher, she'll let you do it in private where no one can see." How awful to be worried you might be teased for crying about your dead mother. "And your daddy can go up with you, go speak to your teachers and principal."

Not that they didn't already know.

She needed this, though, to get back into her routine. Rebecca was dead, but Sarah wasn't. "Did you want me to braid this or something?"

"Do you know how?"

"I can do regular braids, and I can do french braids, and I can do fishtail braids." He'd watched YouTube videos on how to braid hair when Melly's had gotten long enough.

"Yeah? That's cool. Can I have french braids?"

"Sure thing." He parted her hair down the middle and began working the left side into the french braids, careful to keep the tension even. If you didn't, they came out wonky, and he didn't know about Sarah, but Melly was prone to crying jags if he didn't get the braids right. "You want to watch a movie after the braids are finished?" He was hoping she'd actually fall asleep if she let herself relax a little.

"Yeah. Yeah, something happy? Not *Moana*."

He had to chuckle at that. Melly and Linds both had that on constant repeat. "You know that one by heart, I bet. How about the Minions movie?" He'd almost suggested *Despicable Me*, but had remembered the little girls without a mom and swerved it to Minions.

"Yeah, I like that one. I like the dinosaur."

"Me too! Do you have a favorite Minion?" He finished the left braid and started on the right.

"Stuart. He plays guitar. I'm learning how. I'm taking lessons. What about those? Dance? Guitar?"

"You'll still get to go to your lessons, honey. We're going to try to make sure everything is as normal as possible." He was glad she was finally talking.

"Even with the babies? I know Daddy and you are busy."

"But we're not so busy that we can't get you to school and your lessons. We're not so busy we can't love you. The more the merrier, I say."

"You didn't expect me," she whispered.

"Yes and no. You were already a part of the family, but we only got to see you every other weekend and most Fridays. Now, while it might be unexpected, we get to see you every day, and seeing as we already loved you, that's a good thing, you know?" So many things to worry about. God knew what else was hiding in her head.

"I miss her. A lot."

What could he say to that? Of course she did and there wasn't a damn thing he could do to change it. "Yeah, I'm sure you do." He hugged her. "And I'm so sorry."

She cried a little, but it eased up quickly this time.

"Do you want me to stay with you while you watch your movie?" he asked.

"Yeah. Please." She wasn't going to be awake more than a minute.

He appreciated the fact that she was willing to let him comfort her. He had a feeling she might not continue to do so as time passed and she filled her teen years with friends and crushes and growing up, so he was going to help her while he could.

"Is your mom still alive? Daddy's isn't."

"She is. She lives in the country on a farm. Next time I take Melly to see her, maybe I can bring you and the triplets too. And your daddy, of course." His mom loved kids, and she was going to be thrilled to call herself grandma to four more.

"Are there horses?" They headed to Sarah's bedroom, and she squeezed his hand when she saw the bed made, the windows opened.

"There aren't any horses, though her neighbor has some. Mom's got a dairy herd and some sheep, goats, and llamas. Oh, and chickens that run around like they own the place." With Dad gone, his mom had hired someone on to take care of the milking and general upkeep.

"Wow. So you were a farmer when you were little?" She cuddled into the blankets.

"I was. I had daily chores and a dog of my own and everything." It hadn't suited him at all. Which was why he was now a city boy.

"We need a cat. Mom was allergic."

"You'd rather have a cat than a dog?" He thought it wouldn't hurt to have an animal or two here. The place was certainly big enough for pets. As long as the triplets weren't allergic. Or Logan. He had no clue if Logan had allergies. How did he not know that? Somehow, it had never come up. Which made him think that Logan didn't.

"Oh, I like dogs too. We could have both. Puppies bite, though, and so I think we should wait for the babies to be a little bigger."

"What a smart girl. You're an excellent big sister." He got her movie set up for her and sat with his back to her headboard, letting her decide if she wanted to cuddle or just sit next to him.

She sat next to him, nibbling on half of her sandwich. Good deal. Washed, fed, they'd talked, and now she'd get some sleep. That was as good as anyone could hope for under the circumstances. She leaned against him, humming along with the Minions.

It was a fun movie, and about halfway through, he realized Sarah had fallen asleep, head lolled to one side, soft little snores sounding at intervals. Poor love was finally asleep.

He turned the sound down on the TV and slipped out of bed. Then he tucked the covers up around her and kissed her forehead. She cuddled in and smiled. Oh. Oh, better.

He hoped it was a good sign. That she had turned some kind of corner.

Dirk headed downstairs, hearing Logan's low lullaby. Someone was awake. He poked his head in the triplets' room to see.

All three of the babies were on the floor on a huge quilt, Logan stretched out with them, singing and playing with toes and fingers.

God, it was moments like these that deepened his love for this man. What an amazing father. He leaned against the doorframe and watched, keeping quiet so he didn't disturb anyone.

"Oh, are you smiling? Sebastian, I knew you'd be the first."

That made Dirk smile and move into the room. He wanted to see that smile.

"Hey, love. They are in glorious moods."

"That's awesome." He joined Logan on the floor. "Sarah had a bath, some food. She's sleeping."

"Oh, good. Thank you. She needs a friend."

"Yeah. She had some questions I think she was scared to ask you."

"Yeah? Like what?"

"Like was she still going to do her lessons and was it okay if she stayed here. She's worried she's going to cry at school and kids will make fun of her. Just stuff, you know? Things that we assumed would happen, she hasn't. I mean, she asked what would happen with her clothes at her mom's place."

"You and I need to talk about that—not Sarah's things, you know we'll bring what she needs—but all the things there."

"I've never been, so I don't know what she's got. I mean, we don't really need anything, do we? But you should make sure there isn't anything special that you'd want to keep. And I think it's important that Sarah has a chance to keep anything she wants. Well, I guess within reason," he added, in case she wanted to move everything over wholesale.

"Yeah—Rebecca had a lot of furniture, kitchen stuff. I suppose once we decide, we'll hire someone to sell it?"

"That makes sense. You always see signs for estate sales and stuff. There's a lot to deal with, isn't there?"

"Yes. Unraveling people's lives is complicated."

He reached out and touched Logan's hand, then wrapped their fingers together and squeezed.

"You okay?" Logan asked. "I know you've had a lot to deal with too."

"Oh, I'm fine. It's you and Sarah who are hurting. The least I could do is be here for the two of you." He brought Logan's hand to his mouth and kissed the knuckles softly, hoping to offer comfort.

"And you've gained another daughter. I'm so glad she wasn't in that car. I keep having nightmares."

"You can't think like that, love. She wasn't in that car. She's alive and safe and upstairs in her bedroom. You have to put what might have been out of your mind and concentrate on what is. I know that isn't easy, but I think it's important to be here, right here."

Especially with their babies so young, needing them so badly.

"Your family needs you present," he reiterated. "All of us." Because he and Melly were a part of Logan's family now too.

"I know. I feel like I haven't seen Miss Mel in days. I miss her bad."

"Why don't we do a picnic at the park tomorrow or something?"

"Do you think the weather is nice enough for the babies? I'd love that."

"It's supposed to be nice tomorrow. And we can bundle them up so they stay warm. I think the girls would love it. Give them something fun." Everything had been wrapped around Rebecca's death since it had happened.

"We'll try it. What can it hurt, right?"

"Yeah. That's what I was thinking." He squeezed Logan's shoulder, then leaned against him as they sat together. They were going to get through this. They were.

Chapter Thirteen

"I'M not going."

Logan clenched his teeth. "Then you can sit in the van quietly while we have our picnic, but you're coming with us."

Sarah crossed her arms and stuck her chin out, looking as stubborn as a mule.

"You have to come," Mel insisted. "We're having a family picnic."

"I don't want to…."

"But we're family! You have to. Please." Mel was already getting teary.

Dirk handed Mel a blanket. "Why don't you find us the best spot to set ourselves up."

She gave Sarah one last, long look and took the blanket to head off on her mission.

Dirk turned to Sarah. "You should come with us. You don't have to eat anything or say anything, but you should come with us."

"Please," Logan added. "For Mel, honey." He knew she had a soft spot a mile wide for her "baby" sister.

"Fine." She glared at him but undid her seat belt and climbed out, stomping in the direction Mel had gone.

Dirk sighed and squeezed his shoulders briefly. "She might not think so, but this is good for her."

"I know. We have to get back to life, right?"

"We do. I know what happened to Rebecca is awful and that everyone misses her terribly. But we're all here and alive and have so much living left to do. Rebecca wouldn't want her baby girl to spend the rest of her life unhappy. I know that. You know that. And somewhere inside, so does Sarah."

Yes, and he thought that was half the trouble. She was beginning to want to have her life back, but she felt guilty about it.

"I hear you. I need to start dealing with the practical nonsense too." He smiled at the babies in the carriage. "But not today."

"Nope. Today is a family picnic. A fun time for the girls. Some sunshine for the babies." Dirk pointed to where Mel had chosen to lay out the blanket, down near the little man-made lake by a tree for shade. Sarah was helping her spread out the blanket, the two of them smoothing out all the folds.

Suzy was awake and looking around, but the boys were sound asleep, Sebastian sucking his thumb. There were parenting books that claimed that was a terrible habit and you had to stop it as soon as you could. Others said the opposite. He thought when you had three of them at once, any self-soothing they could do was a bonus.

Dirk was carrying the picnic basket and the two other bags full of stuff that didn't go into the oversized diaper bag he had hanging off the back of the carriage. He wasn't sure what all Dirk had packed, but for the first time in a while, he was looking forward to eating.

He was hoping for chips and turkey sandwiches with provolone. He liked that it was going to be a surprise, though. It was a reminder that he wasn't in this alone, that he had someone at his back, supporting him.

"All right, this looks like a beautiful spot." Dirk smiled at the girls. "Well done."

"Thank you! Sarah chose it with me."

"I approve. It's a gorgeous day. I missed the sun."

"Why don't the two of you play for a while, and we'll call you back when we've got the picnic set up," Dirk suggested.

"Would you like to go swing, Melly?" Logan asked.

Her little eyes lit up, and she leaped at him. "Yes, please!"

Dirk chuckled. "If she didn't already love you, that would have done the trick. Go on. I'll keep an eye on the babies while I set out the food."

"I'll help Dirk with the triplets, Daddy."

Oh, his dear, good girl. "Thank you, honey. You rock."

He grabbed Melly's hand and grinned at her. "Let's go!"

She held on tight and tugged him along, chattering happily. "I love swings. They're my favorite."

"Oh, me too. I like the merry-go-round and the teeter-totter, but the swings are my favorite."

"The teeter scares me," Mel admitted, letting go of his hand and skipping to the swings.

"Oh, we'll have to get one for you to try for the backyard. Shall we bring the playhouse over too?"

"A playhouse?" Her eyes lit up.

"Yes, there's one in Sarah's old house. We can bring it." Someone should use it. Four someones.

"Yay!" She laughed and kicked her legs. "Swing me, Unca Log, swing me!"

Her happiness was infectious, and he started pushing her, her happy squeals making him grin. Lord, he adored her.

This had been a wonderful idea, and it was a balm to the places that were still sharp with pain.

He could see Dirk and Sarah working on setting out their picnic, and it looked like it was going to be quite the feast.

They could have played until dark, he thought, but when the triplets began to fuss, Melly frowned. "My babies are crying."

"Are they? Your da and Sarah have them."

"I'll check them," she announced, flying off the swing without letting it stop, which propelled her forward several quick steps, and she turned it into a run, heading right for "her" babies.

He followed her, totally stunned by her determination, her absolute love for the triplets.

She went to the carriage and petted each of their bellies. "It's okay, babies. I'm here."

Suzy flailed, hands grabbing at Melly's arm.

"Hi, Suzy-baby. It's Melly." She let Suzy wrap her hand around her index finger. "See, she knows me."

Dirk rubbed his hand through Mel's hair. "She does, honey."

"Of course she does. You're her family." Sarah sighed softly, and Logan went to her. "And you're our family, honey."

"I miss her, Daddy."

"Me too." And that was that. Him too.

She leaned against him, and he hugged her tight.

Dirk gave him a sympathetic smile. "Lunch is ready whenever you guys are."

"What did you bring to eat, honey?"

"There's turkey sandwiches, and cheese sandwiches for the girls. And potato chips. And carrot sticks. Oh, and juice boxes."

"Rock on. Sandwiches!" He peeked into the stroller and nuzzled baby bellies.

Dirk laughed softly and handed him a sandwich, then offered cheese sandwiches to the girls.

"Sweet! This is a great spread, love. Thank you."

"You're welcome." Dirk smiled warmly and took a bite out of his own sandwich. He tilted his head back as he chewed, face in the sun, looking happy.

"Love? Are you two boyfriends?" Sarah looked at them, one after the other.

It was Dirk who answered her, not apologetically or diffidently at all—the simple truth. "We are. We have been for a while."

"Are you going to get married? Are you going to adopt the babies and Melly?"

Logan found himself speechless and staring.

Dirk chuckled. "That's a lot of questions that we haven't discussed together yet. But it's okay to ask about it. It's okay to ask about anything that you have questions about. Would you like us to all be one big family?"

"I would! I could have two daddies and two sisters and two brothers!" Melly bounced, making the babies squeal with laughter.

Dirk grinned at his daughter before turning to look at Logan, warmth in his eyes. "We'll have to talk about it."

"We will. Later. Right now we're having a picnic." Logan hadn't had any time to consider things like long-term, marriage.

But his daughter had clearly been thinking big thoughts.

"We're having a great picnic," Dirk declared.

"A perfect one. I have all my kiddos, Dirk, and sandwiches."

Dirk leaned over and kissed him on the cheek. "Love you, Logan."

"I love you too."

Sarah groaned. "Stop it."

Dirk made a hiccuping sound, which Logan assumed was him swallowing his laughter at Sarah's reaction.

"Oh, Dirky-Worky! I adore you." He started peppering Dirk's face with kisses.

"Ewww!" Sarah made a gagging noise, and Dirk lost it, laughing hard.

"Dirky-Worky Daddy!" Melly danced around singing.

Dirk narrowed his eyes at Logan. "Oh, you are in so much trouble."

Sarah began to giggle, the sound so damn welcome.

He saw Dirk's eyes light up, but Dirk didn't give away how happy he was at Sarah's soft laughter, not making a big deal of the moment.

"I suppose I'll have to come up with something that rhymes with Logan, won't I? Loggy-Woggy?"

"That doesn't rhyme. At all."

"It does too!" Dirk repeated it. "Loggy-Woggy. It totally rhymes."

"It doesn't rhyme with Logan, Dirky-Worky." He couldn't stop laughing, and the kids were right behind.

"But worky doesn't rhyme at all with Dirk!" Poor Dirk looked like a goldfish, gasping for breath.

"Dirky-Worky *Daddy*!" Melly insisted.

Dirk's expression melted into a smile, and he opened his arms, Melly pushing into them. "I love you, Melly girl."

"Love you, Da. I do." She kissed him back and settled in his lap. Dirk kissed the top of her head and looped an arm around her, settling easily with her.

He shot Logan a smile, one full of warmth and happiness that seemed to settle over their picnic like a blanket. Even Sarah seemed to have turned a corner in her grief.

This had been a good idea.

Hopefully they'd have lots more to come.

Chapter Fourteen

DIRK was exhausted. His feet were tired, his brain was tired—hell, his fingers were tired. But Rebecca's place had been cleared out, the last of the stuff that hadn't sold packed up and sent to a thrift store.

Sarah had the stuff she'd wanted. It was mostly still in boxes in one of the extra bedrooms, waiting for her to be ready to go through it.

Melly was finally down for the count, Sarah up in her room with a movie. And the triplets were currently quiet. Maybe he could close his eyes and get a nap. Maybe he'd do it right here on the couch where he'd landed.

Logan was in the kitchen, putting things away, singing along with the radio.

It felt good to hear. Now that the estate was settled, something had eased in Logan. That was cool.

They'd brought back a ton of toys, including a lot of things designed for backyard play. Melly was over the moon. Dirk wasn't ever going to be able to thank Logan enough for the things he'd done for Dirk and Melly.

"Hey," he called out softly. "Did I tell you today how much I love you?"

"Hey. You want a beer?"

"Sure, I'll have a beer. Though I have to warn you that I might fall asleep if I do."

"That's okay." Logan came out of the kitchen with two bottles. "I don't blame you."

His lover looked as tired as he was.

He patted the couch next to him. "Sit with me."

"I'm almost done with the kitchen." Logan plopped down. "How's Melly doing?"

"Dead asleep. She outdid herself today. I even found her dragging this huge box, all by herself. It was adorable."

"Aw. She was so excited by the playhouse. I'll have someone come and anchor the jungle gym next week."

"She thinks she's won the lottery. Babies and a jungle gym in the backyard." Dirk thought he'd won the lottery too. Four new kids and this beautiful man. Not to mention a house to live in.

"She was telling me she wants to grow flowers and a garden. She's so excited by the thought that the yard is ours."

That sounded so much like his girl, and Dirk smiled. "She's got a huge heart, my girl."

"God yes. So does Sarah, and you'll get to see it. She's kind and smart as a whip."

"I know. She's just having a rough time. It's totally understandable."

"It is." Logan leaned against him. "But I wanted you to know."

"I know, love. I'm not judging her badly, I promise." He adored Sarah. She was a kid who had been dealt a harsh blow, and she was theirs. Their oldest.

He wound his fingers with Logan's and took a sip of his beer. "So that's the bulk of what needed doing actually done now, right?"

"I think so? I mean, I should do more while they're all resting, but…."

Dirk snorted. "You look like I feel, so I think resting and possibly sleeping is what you should be doing while all five kids are quiet and happy without us. The house closes next week, right? And then it's not your responsibility anymore." He knew Logan had enough on his plate with his daughter and the triplets—he didn't need all this other shit pulling at his time as well.

"Thank God. I mean, I'm incredibly grateful for the insurance money and the house. If we invest carefully, we'll be able to send all the kids to school with what there is." Logan said that so casually, but did he mean Melly too?

Dirk thought about it for a time, then figured he would come out and ask. They hadn't entirely sorted out the money issue. At least he didn't feel like they had. The whole thing where he and Melly lived here and were kept in food and clothes and he was the de facto nanny was great, was amazing. But as he wasn't actually making money, he couldn't save for her college. "All five of the kids?"

"Of course." The immediacy of the answer made him shiver. "I mean, if it's okay with you."

When it came to Melly's future, he had no shame. "It's absolutely okay. Thank you so much."

"Rebecca knew how much I care about you and Mel. She would have approved."

He squeezed Logan's hand. "It worries me sometimes that I'm not bringing in any money at all. I don't want you to think that that's why I'm here with you."

"I don't want you to be without money, either, you know? I worry that you'll feel like I control everything."

He nodded. He'd thought about that too. That he'd eventually feel like Logan had all the power. He didn't now, but in ten years? Twenty?

Logan held his head. "I'm not sure how to make that work. I mean, couples have, right? For decades."

Dirk chuckled. "Yeah, yeah, they have. One breadwinner, and it works. Is this you asking me to marry you?" Because that was usually the paperwork involved.

"Do you want to? I mean, get married?"

"I want to be a family with you. The paperwork would be to protect us from outside assholes down the line."

"You know I appreciate paperwork."

He laughed, honestly tickled by the words. "You do. Look, I've been ready to hitch my wagon to yours since before I moved in here. Hell, since before you got the triplets if I'm honest. I've been halfway in love with you ever since we first met at the coffeehouse." He was a dweeb and he knew it, but his gut had totally been right.

"You never let on, honey. Am I that scary?"

"Would you have believed me that early on? When we first met? And I sure would have looked like a money grubber. You needed to get to know me without that kind of baggage first."

"I wouldn't! You're a good dad!" Logan looked at him like he was insane.

"That's part of why I love you, eh? You see the good things about me."

"That's easy." Logan leaned over and kissed him, nice and slowly.

He hummed softly, the kiss lazy and sweet. There wasn't a hurry, a need to get hot and bothered. It was the intimacy that felt so good. He loved being close with Logan. He loved the steady way they'd built a life together. How well they were handling the upheaval of Sarah's life and the loss of her mother was proof of that in his eyes.

He slid his hand around Logan's head, cupping it as they continued their soft explorations.

Logan smiled against his lips, hummed for him, and almost crawled into his lap. Desire flared in his belly, made his balls ache and his prick try to come to life despite his exhaustion. He wrapped his arms around Logan, the tiredness sloughing off the longer they kissed.

"Dirk. Honey. Bedroom?"

"Uh-huh." He didn't want to get up and move, but there were kids here, and the grown-ups needed a door they could close.

Before he could voice any of that, one of the babies started whining. He closed his eyes. "Maybe if we're very quiet, like very, he'll go back to sleep."

"Maybe. Or I can go pat his back a minute, if not."

"Yeah, the eternal choice. Do you leave him be to see if he'll self-soothe and go back to sleep, or do you go and help him along so he doesn't wake his siblings?" Dirk chuckled. He was pretty sure that was

Seb, who'd been the first to discover his thumb, so they had a chance.

The baby muttered and cooed; then the sounds became muffled and slowly stopped.

He gave Logan a grin. "I think we can risk it, don't you?" They could make a mad—quiet—dash to the bedroom. It made him feel almost like a teenager again. Almost.

"The next twenty years are going to be like this, aren't they?"

"From your lips to God's ears." He thought having this to look forward to for that long was amazing.

Logan chuckled, the sound quiet but so merry. It made Dirk smile and bring their lips back together again. They really did need to move to the bedroom, but this felt wonderful.

Logan's kisses made him a little dizzy. His fiancé's kisses. His fiancé… oh, he liked the sound of that. He liked how it made him feel.

His fiancé. His family. His babies.

Lord, he sounded like Melly.

"You make me happy, Logan. Truly."

"Good. It would be awful if you didn't like me."

"I wouldn't be here if I didn't!" He laughed and hugged Logan tight. "I'll have to give you more compliments so you're better at getting them."

"Come to bed, lover. It's been a crazy day."

"It's been an exhausting day, but good. You can move forward now. You and Sarah." He waited for Logan to get up, then stood himself.

"All of us. Even the triplets."

He wasn't sure the triplets had noticed anything, but he nodded along. "Even the triplets."

"They say babies can feel stress, right?"

"They have been more fractious over the last few weeks," Dirk noted.

"I can't believe how fast they're growing."

Dirk looked at Logan. "Why are we talking about the kids?"

Logan blinked at him a few times. "I don't know, why?"

Dirk laughed and shook his head. "Because they take up so much of our time and thoughts that it's our new normal, maybe. Come on, take me upstairs to bed and make love with me before anyone wakes up."

"God yes. Please. Let's share orgasms."

"We'll peek in on Melly and triplets as we go by. Then we'll lock our door." He took Logan's hand and led his lover and soon-to-be husband up to their bedroom. God willing they'd have enough time to make each other feel amazing before any of their little ones needed attention.

Chapter Fifteen

"YOU did what?" Zack stared at him.

"I think I asked him to marry me." Logan grinned. "Hazelnut-and-white-chocolate latte, please."

"Emily, make Logan a hazelnut-and-white-chocolate latte, please, and bring it over to us." Zack grabbed his own coffee in one hand, Logan's arm in the other, and marched him over to their usual table.

It was a little strange to be sitting here without any of the others, but he'd wanted to share the news with his friends and he wasn't planning to be at the Teddy Bear Club meeting, so he'd come to the Roasty Bean early to tell Zack.

"Okay," Zack said as they sat. "Spill."

"We were talking about long-term, about family, and Dirk asked if I was asking him to marry me, and I said I thought so."

Zack snorted. "That's just dripping with romance, my friend. Dripping."

"I know. I had just moved all the stuff from Rebecca's over, we were both exhausted, and the kids were all asleep."

Zack stared at him for a moment after he'd finished speaking, then poked him in the side. "Well? Don't keep me in suspense—did he say yes?"

"Yeah. He really did." And Logan wasn't sure how that happened.

"So this is good news? Or are you having regrets now that you're not exhausted and stressed?"

"No regrets here. Dirk's solid—a good dad, a good guy." Wait, that didn't sound sparkly.

It seemed that Zack agreed with his last thought. "Solid. Honey, I'm not being a bitch, but do you love him?"

"I do. I mean, I genuinely do. He's magical. He's who I need." And if he was too tired and sad to be googly-eyed, sue him.

"That was much more convincing." Zack kissed his cheek. "And I'm happy for you, hon, I really am. So when do I need to plan the wedding for?"

"I don't know. I'll have to talk to my affianced." Oh, that was fun to say. "Maybe Christmas? A lot will depend on Sarah, I think."

"Affianced? Aren't you fancy!" Zack chuckled but sobered fairly quickly. "Yeah, it might be weird for her if you got married so soon after Rebecca passed away." Zack squeezed his arm. "You will have to discuss it with your fancy man."

"And with our family, right?" That was how this was supposed to happen.

Zack looked very pleased about that. "Can I spill your beans once everyone is here today? It'll be great to have such a happy occasion to look forward to."

"Yeah. Let me call Dirk. Maybe we can have everyone over for a cookout this weekend to celebrate."

"That would be lovely. We could all help get the backyard play stuff set up properly too."

Emily called for Zack, and he glanced back at her and nodded. "Okay, I have to go help until we all meet up. Call your man and warn him I won't be able to keep my mouth shut." Zack leaned over and gave him a hug.

"Fair enough." He called home to check on his family and his lover.

Dirk answered after the second ring. "Hey, babe. What's up?"

"Hey you. How's it going?" *Are you ready for company?*

"I'm great, and the kids are awesome. Melly and I are having blanket time with the three esses."

"Oh, as soon as Sarah's done with her guitar lessons and I pick up pizza, we'll be home. The guys want to come this weekend and celebrate our engagement. You interested?"

"Yeah, really? That sounds like fun!"

"Cool. I'm going to have to tell Sarah about this, you know? About us."

"Of course we are. I'm hoping she'll be happy for us. You never know how she's going to react, though. Especially so soon after Rebecca. Don't be mad at her if she's not happy for us to start with."

"I won't be. Zack is. Happy, that is."

"Yeah? That's awesome. I just need to pass the test with Aiden, eh?" Dirk chuckled, but it didn't really seem like he was joking. "Are you staying for the

Teddy Bear Club meeting? I'm looking forward to the triplets being a little bit older so we can bring them and attend together."

"I'm not, no. I'll pick up Sarah and supper, and I'll be home." He didn't want to leave Dirk to deal on his own.

"Ooh. Are we having fried chicken for supper?" Dirk licked his lips audibly. What a crazy sound.

He'd thought pizza, but fried chicken worked for him. "With mashed potatoes and gravy or onion rings?"

"Yes, please." There was a thread of laughter in Dirk's voice. "That means get both, please. And if you pick it up from the place on Fourth, they have biscuits too...."

"I'm on it. Dessert?"

"Ooh." Dirk lowered his voice. "Surprise me."

Was his fiancé flirting with him?

"I'll see if I can find something yummy." God, that made him a bit squirmy.

"And I'll see if I can find a bit of time to thank you appropriately." Definitely flirting.

"I'll grab doughnuts."

Dirk laughed softly. "You and your doughnuts. I thought you were going to surprise me?"

Dammit. "You don't know which ones I'm going to choose...."

"I guess that's true. Okay, you saved yourself there." Dirk chuckled again. "I'll see you later, Loggy-Woggy."

"Yeah, yeah, yeah. I'll see you soon." God, Dirk made him smile.

"Look at you," Zack said after Logan had hung up. Zack offered him another cup of coffee. "Now that is the look of a man in love."

"Is it?" He drank deep, liking the idea of that.

"Oh yes, indeed it is."

"Good. I want it obvious. I need to let Sarah know next."

"Yeah, she should know before the world does." Zack gave him a hug. "I will try not to spill the beans to Aiden and Dev, but I can't make you any promises."

"Oh. Oh! Dirk says Saturday sounds great." He ought to have Sarah invite both of her best friends. That would make her feel more included, he thought.

"The girls and I will be thrilled to be there. What do you need me to bring?"

"Dessert?" Zack had access to the best bakery goods.

"You've got it. I'll bring some yummy stuff."

"Rock on. I'll provide burgers and dogs and all that stuff."

"You provide what you like, but I have to tell you the twins are not going to eat dogs. They'll have very strong feelings about that, actually." Zack's eyes twinkled wickedly. "They might even call the SPCA on you if you're serving dogs."

"Shut up, butthead." He popped Zack on the chest even as he laughed.

"Hey, you're the one who said you were serving dog." Zack ducked out of the way of Logan's arm as he swung again, also laughing. "Go on. We'll see you on Saturday."

"Let's shoot for noonish. Playclothes."

"Yeah, yeah, you're going to make us work. Got it." Zack was still laughing as he backed toward the counter.

Logan grabbed his cup and headed out to get Sarah. It was a little walk, and he enjoyed the warmth.

He needed to talk to his daughter, feel her out about Dirk. He thought the Olde Shoppe on Fifth would be a good spot to sit and have a chat together, with ice cream to grease the skids. Then they could pick up supper and dessert and head home.

Sarah came running out to him almost as soon as the bell rang, her little hand slipping into his. "It's Friday! No school for a whole weekend!"

"Hooray! How was your day, sweetie?"

She wrinkled her nose. "A little bit stinky."

"Stinky?"

"Uh-huh. Jordan and Ricky called me a crybaby. I wanted to kick them, but you and Mommy said hitting is wrong and I think kicking is like hitting, so I didn't."

"Good girl. Jordan and Ricky are obviously turds, while you are a classy, educated girl."

She giggled at him. "You called them turds!"

"I did." And he'd do it again if he had to.

"Isn't that a bad word, Daddy?" she asked as they walked toward the ice cream shop.

"It's sort of bad, and it's ugly."

She frowned, and he could almost see the wheels turning in her head as she worked that one out. "And it's okay to call them that because they're ugly."

"Yes, but you might not do that at school, hmm?"

"Like no hitting?" She thought for another minute. "Okay."

They got to the little store and went in, Sarah's attention suddenly on the tubs of ice cream.

"Look at it all, Daddy."

"I know, right? Are you going to get different flavors or two scoops of the same?"

She licked her lips a few times, then straightened her spine, telling him she'd made a decision. "I'm getting chocolate heaven and very vanilla." Then she turned to look at him. "Can I have whipped cream and sprinkles on it too, please?"

"Sure. I'm going to have the very same thing, I think. With peanuts too."

"I don't want peanuts. Can I have marshmallow fluff instead?"

He appreciated the fact she was a negotiator. She got that from him.

"You can." He hugged her. God, he loved her, so much.

They ordered their ice creams, and he paid. Once they'd picked up their bowls, they went and sat at a little table in the corner together.

She jabbered about her day—about art class and music, about the upcoming science fair.

Going back to school had been the best thing for her. It gave her a routine, things to do other than wallow in her mother having died. He was glad. He'd been worried about her coming back from it, but he thought it was going to be okay. She still had her moments, of course, but they'd turned a corner.

When she'd talked herself out, he took his chance. "So, I need to talk with you about something."

"Uh-huh?" She shoved another spoonful of ice cream into her mouth.

"What do you think about me and Dirk getting married?"

"Because Mommy went to heaven?"

"No. No, your mom and I were never going to get married. I want to marry Dirk because I love him, and I want us to be an official family."

She met his gaze head-on. "What about me?"

What the hell did that mean? "What are you asking, baby?"

"If you have a new family, what about me?"

"Oh baby." God, kids worried about the strangest things. At least she trusted him enough to talk to him, right? "You will always, always be my family. You will always be the triplets' family. I think you're already Dirk and Melly's family. This is a legal contract between us, joining our families together."

"So I get two daddies?"

"Yes. And another sister."

"What if I didn't want you to?"

"Then we'd have to talk about it, about why you felt that way. I want you to be happy, and this is your home." And he knew that Sarah cared for Dirk and adored Melly.

"Okay." She went back to eating her ice cream like that was that.

"So... is it cool with you?"

"Uh-huh. I like Dirk and Melly."

"Me too. So I was thinking about having a cookout Saturday with the guys. You want to invite your posse? They could sleep over." She hadn't had friends over since Rebecca had died.

"My posse? Oh, Daddy." She giggled at him, making him suddenly feel impossibly old for a moment.

"Your gang? Your herd?" He could get worse.

She laughed harder. "No! They're my friends!"

"Okay. Shall we invite them for a sleepover Saturday?" Silly girl.

She nodded. "Can we stay up really late and have pizza delivered?"

"Well, I'm going to make hamburgers and hot dogs, but I suppose we can do that, yes." Lord, those girls and their pizzas.

"I mean, have the pizza really late—after supper. Like when it's dark out." Her eyes shone with excitement.

"Oh. I see. After normal bedtime and everything." God, he remembered that, being so excited to stay up late, to get a hint of being a grown-up.

She nodded, almost bouncing in her chair. "Can I have Cassie and Elena and Anita *and* Belinda?"

"Of course. But—" He held up one finger. "—you guys have to be nice to Melly and be quiet when the babies are sleeping. Fair?"

She nodded. "We'll be good, Daddy, I promise." She chattered at him, talking excitedly about all the things they were going to do.

"Well, I think we should go pick up some groceries and then grab dinner for Dirk and Melly and us, what do you think?"

"Can we get chicken for dinner? Dirk really likes chicken."

"We can. That sounds great." Oh, he was over the moon.

She made him so proud.

They headed for the grocery store, Sarah continuing to tell him all about tomorrow. Lord, it was going to be a busy day. Busy, but good.

Chapter Sixteen

DIRK loved taking care of the triplets. He could tell them apart by sight now, and usually by their cry. He also got to stay home with Melly this way. It really was a dream—a new home, a new man, a house full of love. He didn't even have to worry about what they were going to do for supper tonight because Logan was bringing home chicken. It didn't get much better than that.

He and Melly were currently playing peekaboo with the babies. The triplets were in their bouncy chairs on the floor, giggling like crazy any time they were peekabooed. It was the cutest thing in the world, and he hoped Logan got home soon so he could share in it.

Melly heard the garage door before he did. "Da! They're home!"

The babies sensed Mel's excitement and began hooting and kicking.

"So they are. You gonna go welcome them home?" He was excited himself. He loved it when they were all home together. He watched Melly bound away, all eagerness and happiness. Being here with Logan, Sarah, and the babies was a wonderful boon for her. Melly was thriving as a sibling.

"Sarah! Sarah, the babies are playing peekyboo!"

"Yeah? We bought groceries. There's lots. Can you help Daddy carry too?"

"Yes! I help!" That was his Melly, always willing to do her part.

"Welcome home, Sarah and Logan," he called out. "Do you need my help too?" The babies would be fine for two minutes if Logan needed him to fetch and carry. He made faces at Suzy, who laughed and kicked for him.

"Yes please. I'll watch the babies." Sarah came in with a smile. "Daddy is letting me have a slumber party tomorrow."

"Oh wow, how great is that?" Dirk had a feeling the word slumber was a misnomer, but he figured as long as they didn't wake the babies, they could sleep the next day. He tousled her hair and went for the garage, grinning at Melly as she passed him carrying a bag that was almost as big as she was. He could see bread sticking out of the top of it, though, and knew it wasn't very heavy.

"Hey," he said as he walked into the garage. "I have been informed there's groceries to help carry."

"Why yes. And there is supper and dessert as well." Logan was beaming. Simply beaming.

"Oh, you're in a good mood." He went up to Logan and kissed him gently.

"I spoke to my oldest daughter about us getting married, and she approved. So I supposed we ought to speak to Melly."

"Oh." Pleasure went through him. They'd talked about it, and Logan had asked him, but this was totally proactive on Logan's part and made it more real. He leaned in and took another kiss, this one lingering.

"Mmm... hey, lover." Logan rubbed their noses together, smiling at him, until Melly came stomping in.

"Groceries. Supper. No kissing!"

He laughed and rubbed Logan's nose. "Yes, bossy."

"Da! No kissing. Chicken."

"Someone is hungry," he noted, giving Logan a warm smile. "Do you think there's a piece for you in the box?" She loved the drumsticks and the wings.

"Uh-huh. I want the drumstick!"

"Oh?" He feigned surprise. "And are you going to play the drums with it?"

"Da! No. You can't play music with food!"

He chuckled as he carried his load of groceries into the kitchen. Logan made another three trips. Lord, the man had bought the entire store.

"Just how many people are coming to this shindig tomorrow?" he asked as he pulled some paper plates out of the cupboard—there was no reason to make dirty dishes for takeout, right?

"Zack and the twins, Aiden and Dev and their babies. Us. Sarah invited four friends, and I offered to feed their families. Everyone's bringing something to share."

"I'm not sure they needed to. I think you bought out the entire grocery store," he teased. He bumped their hips together. "We gonna eat in the front room with the babies? Oh! You have to see them when you play peekaboo with them. It's the cutest thing ever."

"We are. Do you have bottles made, or do I need to make some up?" Logan was surprisingly easy about the thought of never again eating without feeding a baby at the same time. He proved every day what a great dad he was.

"They're made up and in the front room. I figured they were going to get hungry around the same time they stopped wanting to play." He searched the bags and grabbed the ones with their supper. He stuffed the paper plates into it, along with a bunch of napkins and some plastic cups. There. Easy to carry.

"Let's go, boys!" Melly proclaimed, marching her way down the hall.

He met Logan's gaze. "See? She's very bossy."

"She knows what she wants, that's all."

"I didn't say it was a bad thing. It's just a thing. I actually like it. She's a strong girl."

"She is. She's amazing." Logan sat down and took Sebastian up. "And you're amazing, baby boy."

Seb kicked and drooled, making Dirk grin. They were in such a good mood at the moment. They loved playtime.

Logan got all three babies out of their swings while he dished up food. Onion rings. Uhn. And mashed potatoes and gravy. Corn and biscuits. Logan was good to him. Or at least good to his stomach.

"So, you're going to marry my dad?" Sarah took a piece of breast and put onion rings on.

He glanced at Melly, but her attention was split between her food and the babies. He looked back at Sarah. "I am. Is that okay with you?"

"Yeah. Yeah, I guess. I'm still part of the family, though."

"Of course you are. I'm marrying your daddy, but that means I get all four kids as a part of the family too. Me and Melly get to be family with all of you."

She watched him carefully, sizing him up. He didn't hurry her. She needed to see him, to realize his being there was a good thing. That they really could be a family all together. He just hoped it wasn't too soon after losing her mom.

"Okay. I don't want to change my name, though, okay?"

"That's just fine. I don't think any of us are changing our names...." They hadn't talked about it, but he couldn't see why they would need to change any names. They all belonged to each other no matter what their names were or who was biologically related to who.

They were going to be a family.

"What are you talking about?" Melly asked.

"Our dads getting married."

Well, he supposed that was as good a way as any to let her know. "Me and Uncle Logan. So that we can all be a family. You, Sarah, the babies, Logan, and me. Doesn't that sound good?"

"Does that mean Unca Logan can be my daddy too?"

"Yeah, it does. It means you have two daddies. I think that's pretty special." He looked over at Logan and smiled at his lover. His fiancé.

"Then you can be Daddy Logan!" She plopped down next to Sarah. "Did you hear?"

Sarah snorted. "Uh-huh."

"Can you make me a plate?" Logan asked as he grabbed the bottles and fed all three triplets at once. He was getting to be really good at that.

"Of course. Onion rings or mashed potatoes and gravy?" Of course Dirk was having both, but he knew Logan loved onion rings. Like his daughter. Or maybe Sarah followed after Logan. Either way, they both loved onion rings.

"Onion rings, please."

"Mashed tatoes for me, Da!"

"I know, Melly. With a well in the middle of them to put the gravy." He prepped a plate with the drumstick and the mashed potatoes and gravy for his daughter, adding a biscuit. Then he prepped a plate for Logan, two pieces of white meat, a pile of onion rings, and a biscuit. He gave Melly her plate and set Logan's next to him. "Let me know if you want any help with the burping."

"Suzy's ready for you, if you don't mind."

"I don't." He grabbed the little girl and put her over his shoulder, patting her back gently. "Do you think she's going to give us a good one today, Melly?"

"Maybe. She's sucking on her fist, Da."

Sarah grinned. "You pay good attention, Melly."

"They're my babies."

"Are you still hungry, Suzy?" He shifted her so he could take her fist out of her mouth. "How about a burp, and then we can see if you want a little bit of that rice cereal, okay?"

"Don't forget to eat, Dirk. I can help." Logan's gaze was loving, fond.

"Don't worry. You brought me chicken. I will enjoy it once Suzy's decided not to eat herself." He winked and grabbed a thigh, taking a big bite out of it. The salty crunch was most satisfying.

Together they all managed to eat, five kids and two dads, and it was lovely. They were having a Friday night picnic.

"Someone promised me dessert," he noted.

"Did I?" Butter wouldn't melt in Logan's mouth.

"You very definitely did. And I know you won't disappoint me." He hoped this was coming off as flirting. It had been so long since he'd tried it.

"I won't." Logan grinned, two babies sleeping on his chest. "Sarah, can you grab the box?"

He beamed. He did love dessert. Was the box full of doughnuts? Or was there something else?

"On it, Daddy." Sarah hopped up, hurrying out.

"Looks like both girls are good with the whole marrying thing, eh?" He grinned. "We're going to be a family. A real, legal family."

"I'm sure there will be road bumps, but yes. Yes, we're going to be a real, legal family of seven."

"Seven." He laughed softly. "That's a big number."

Sarah came back to the front room with a box and handed it to Dirk. The chocolate mousse cake smelled like pure heaven. "Oh wow. Wow." He laughed happily, and Suzy shifted in his arms. "Chocolate mousse cake, little girl. You'll find out how great that is one day. You rock, Logan."

"Sarah picked it out. Also, there are a dozen cupcakes for the girls."

"You rock." He blew Logan a kiss, feeling pretty damn awesome at the moment.

"I have doughnuts for the morning." Logan winked at him playfully.

"Oh, I do love a sweet breakfast. Or maybe midnight snack?" He did enjoy the times when they both got up to feed the triplets and got them back to sleep quickly. They'd often make themselves hot chocolate or tea and have something sweet with it. Those times were precious.

"I bought three dozen."

"The man after my heart." He was pretty sure Logan knew what his favorite flavors were too.

"I know how to make my man happy."

"You do." He met Logan's gaze and held it. Then Suzy split the air with her angry little cry that meant she needed a diaper change, and the gooey moment disappeared like that.

They were fathers first, after all. And he wouldn't have it any other way. He'd fallen in love with Logan while the man was a father. It was an important part of his and Logan's identities as far as he was concerned.

He popped up and grabbed Suzy. "You finish your supper, and I'll change Ms. Stinky Bottom."

"Are you sure?"

"Uh-huh." He took her to the powder room at the back of the front room and laid her on the changing table he'd brought down here. There was room, and it made far more sense to have a changing station on each floor.

He talked to her as he changed her poopy diaper, telling her she had a great digestive system, cracking himself up. In no time at all, they were making their way back to chocolate mousse cake.

Logan was holding Melly and the boys, and Sarah was cracking up, laughing hard at them all.

What a beautiful picture. He watched for a moment, committing it to memory. Suzy heard the laughter and wriggled, tried to turn her face so she could see. Dirk brought her over to the others, and he sat next to Logan.

Logan leaned hard. "All clean?"

"Yep. Clean, fed. I imagine she'll be going down soon. I had them up and active for a while before you guys came home." He was trying to tire them out more so they would sleep longer than a couple hours at a time.

"Melly was telling us all about it." Logan grinned, then took a gentle, quick kiss. "She's quite a storyteller, our Mel."

"She is. You are, Melly girl. And she had the triplets laughing and kicking."

"My babies like my stories!"

"They're my babies too, you know." Sarah took Suzy from him, cradling her.

Melly thought really hard on that for several moments, and Dirk had to admit, if only to himself, that he wasn't entirely sure which way she was going to go. Finally, she answered.

"Uh-huh. There's three; that's enough to share."

"Can I have Suzy?"

"Are you going to make her live in your room? That's a lot of stairs." Now Mel looked worried.

Dirk had to swallow his laughter, and when he glanced at Logan, he had to bite the inside of his lip to keep the chuckles in.

"Hey, girls, you know that all three babies are your siblings, right? You don't have to claim any one of them. They are all yours. They are so lucky that they've got two amazing big sisters, and all three of them will need both of you at one point or another, okay?"

Sarah shot him a look that only a preteen girl could, but she was nice or polite enough not to argue in front of Melly.

Okay, so maybe not everything was hunky-dory in the one-big-happy-family department. But he wasn't sure how to fix it, so for now he concentrated on his dessert, though he had to admit, his enjoyment level had dropped some.

Logan nudged his shoulder. "Hormones. We're beginning to experience hormones."

Yeah. And stress. And hell, she didn't upset Melly, did she? She could have needled Mel until she cried.

He smiled, forcing himself to get most, if not all, of his good mood back. "Have you played peekaboo with her yet, Sarah? It'll make her laugh."

"Yeah?"

"Uh-huh. I'll show you." Melly did an exaggerated peekaboo, and Suzy just cracked up, her brothers struggling to see what was funny.

Sarah looked at Suzy and began to giggle, the sound sweet and happy. "Do it again, Mel."

Oh, that was better. This was what being a family was about.

Melly did it once again, and Logan was forced to shift so Seb and Sam could see what was going on. All three laughed together when Melly did it a third time.

"Okay. Let me try." Sarah did it, and Sam farted. Loud.

They were all silent for about a second, maybe even two. Then they all burst out into laughter, and all three babies cooed and kicked, picking up on their laughter and echoing it.

Sarah grinned at him, and he blew a raspberry at her, sending her into another giggle fit.

The whole room was filled with laughter, with joy. Dirk knew it wouldn't last, that there were going to be hard times to come, but right at this very moment, everything was perfect. And he was going to hold on to that as long as he could.

Chapter Seventeen

LOGAN worked robotically through the 3:00 a.m. feeding. Bottles. Burping. Diapers. He had no idea which baby he was dealing with. He just worked, humming the entire time.

When he was done, he discovered Dirk in the doorway with a couple of mugs that he knew contained hot cocoa. "There's cookies on the table between the love seats in our room."

"Are there?" he whispered back. He loved these private, stolen times.

"Uh-huh." Dirk began to walk slowly backward, holding the large mugs out like a beacon. "You know you want to come and get it."

He fought his laughter, because he didn't want those babies to wake up. "I totally do. Totally."

"Good." Dirk glanced behind him, then continued walking backward before turning into their room. Logan could see flames flickering in the fireplace, and a plate of oatmeal-chocolate-chip cookies graced the table between the two love seats.

Oh, look at that. How lovely. "Thank you, love."

"Come on." Dirk handed him one of the mugs and settled on a love seat. Dirk held out his arm. "There's a you-shaped spot right here."

"Mmm…." He cuddled in, leaning hard against his fiancé. Very nice.

"Yeah. You fit so perfectly." Dirk kissed the top of his head.

"How're you doing, honey?" He was tired, but satisfied, which was basically how his days worked.

"I'm great. Did you hear the babies laughing today? Like honest-to-god laughing. It does my heart good to hear that sound. Supper was so much fun."

"Yeah, and Sarah was trying hard to be a part of everything too. I was so proud of her."

"She's doing good. I think we're going to have some moments, but we were going to have that anyway. She is almost a teenager, after all." Dirk's voice flowed over him, warm and soft.

"Watch your mouth," he teased. Kids weren't perfect, and blended families could be tough.

"I'd rather watch yours," Dirk murmured, the tenor of his voice dropping.

"Well, listen to you." He leaned forward, eager for a kiss, for a connection.

"Or even better, feel me." Dirk closed the distance between their lips, and the kiss was soft and warm. All good. He sighed, then wrapped one hand around Dirk's shoulder and drew him in closer.

The kiss deepened slowly, naturally, as if they had all the time in the world. Which they did. He loved that about Dirk. When it was just the two of them, he seemed to be able to shut everything out and live in the moment.

Together they breathed and kissed, and it was a little like being teenagers, but better, because they could be lazy.

Dirk ran his hands over Logan's body, the touches as easy and soft as the kisses they shared. His belly tightened, and his breathing sped up. God, that was lovely. Dirk hummed softly, and yeah, things were getting hotter, hunger licking through him. Faster. He didn't say it; he just tugged on Dirk, encouraging him to move.

Groaning, Dirk leaned forward, pressing him down into the cushions of the love seat. He shivered, his body going hard, need sinking into his bones.

"God, I want you, Logan. All the way want you."

He got that. The last time they'd gone to bed to make love they'd been interrupted by babies. The time before that it had been Sarah. He wanted this too. His body wanted it bad.

"Yes, please. It's been so long. You can have anything you want from me."

"I want you to make love to me. I want to feel you inside me."

"Listen to you." Logan groaned and buried his face in Dirk's throat.

"Listen to me and do as I say. You will make love to me," Dirk intoned before smiling and leaning in to nibble at his throat.

Logan nodded and reached down to cup Dirk's balls and roll them. Dirk groaned and jerked toward him.

"Oh God, yes, please."

"Shh…. Don't wake Melly." He rolled again, teasing.

"I'll scream into your skin," Dirk suggested.

"Fair enough." He pushed at Dirk's sleep pants, searching for skin.

Dirk helped, sort of, fumbling at the tie and tearing open the waistband. "Touch me, Logan. You gotta."

"I am. I have you." He pushed into Dirk's pants and wrapped his fingers around Dirk's cock.

Dirk groaned, the sound low and sweet and so needy. It made him feel like a class A stud.

He jacked Dirk, slowly at first, measuring from base to tip. Dirk moaned and muttered, whispering nonsense as he moved his hips, trying to encourage more speed.

"So fucking pretty." He started humping, driving in time with his strokes.

"Not as good-looking as you," Dirk insisted. "You're so hot." The words were quiet, maybe twisted a little, Dirk gasping in between them and pulling in short, sharp breaths.

"And you're mine. God." He wasn't going to make it. He was going to blow.

"Fuck. Oh shit, fuck." The words were filthy and needy, offered freely.

"Naughty, naughty." He laughed softly, driving them harder together.

"Uh. Just…. What?" Dirk was clearly lost in his pleasure and had no idea what he was saying.

"Love you." That was the important part.

"Oh… I love you too." Dirk gave him a goofy smile, then groaned, his eyes rolling back in his head as Logan tugged on his prick. He fumbled his own pants out of the way, gathered Dirk's and his erections both in one hand and pulled, strong and hard.

Dirk kissed him again, lips sliding along his, tongue dipping in to fuck his mouth. Damn, that made the sensations around his prick so much better.

He began to pant, his eyes rolling back in his head.

"Gonna make me come so hard." Dirk gasped the words, body rolling, losing the rhythm they'd found, signaling Logan that Dirk was about to come for him.

"Come on." He jerked, his eyes rolling back in his head.

"Uh-huh." With that Dirk spilled, come spreading between them.

He leaned down, hid his face in Dirk's throat, hand still moving.

"Your turn," murmured Dirk, the sounds vibrating Dirk's throat against his lips.

"Uhn." He didn't have anything else. Not a single word.

"Unless you want to make good on doing me?"

"Dirk!" Oh fuck, he wanted that, but he was so close.

"You gonna stay hard if you come now?" Dirk stared down at him, eyes shining and full of need.

"Sh. Keep me hard? Can you, I mean? God, don't stop."

Dirk laughed, the sound breathless. Sexy. Dirk kept moving against him, gliding their bodies together. "I want you inside me." Dirk pulled Logan's hand off his cock. "I'm serious, love."

Logan reached up and cupped Dirk's cheek. "Then let's slow this down. Just in case I'm not good for a twofer." He didn't want to leave Dirk wanting if his body was too tired to keep going.

"I bet you are, but that's fine. I can take my time." Dirk shifted, moving so they were lying side by side, squished together on the love seat. Then he turned the rubbing into a gentle undulation and kissed Logan, long and sweet, calming things down, making Logan's balls ache.

Dirk grinned at him, the look almost wicked. Naughty boy. His naughty boy.

"You feel so good against me. I love it when I can enjoy it."

"Do you?" He licked his lips, the urge to drive them together so tempting.

Dirk laughed softly. "Maybe we should get to the prepping now. Before you lose it."

"Do we have to go back to the bed?"

"It's been too long for me not to get prepped…."

Logan blinked. "Are you…. Oh God. So hot."

"I have no idea what you mean, but I'm all over you thinking I'm hot."

"Ride me?" He was proud of himself for getting that many words out.

"Soon as you get me wet, I'm gonna ride the hell out of you."

"Slick." Really? All this talking? He was losing his mind.

"Uh-huh. Lube? Vaseline? Saliva? I don't fucking care what, but we need something, babe."

"Side table. Bed. Now." Okay, he was following. He had a plan.

"I thought—" Dirk cut himself off and shook his head. He got off the love seat and held out his hand. "Let's go."

"I did too. I want lube. I want to have the lamp on so I can watch."

"You say the best things," Dirk told him, dragging him over to the bed, both of them nearly tripping over their pajama bottoms as they went. It had them laughing and tugging at each other's clothes. "Wait! We gotta lock the door."

"Get the lube. I'll get the door." He kicked off his pants and managed to hit the lock.

When he turned around, there was Dirk, lying in the middle of the bed, propped up on one elbow, cock pointed right at Logan, the lube in one hand.

"Mmm... look at you. You make a pretty picture."

"I don't want you to just look at me, though. I want you to ravish me."

He chuckled softly, then pounced, tackling his lover. Dirk's happy laughter was smothered by his kisses. Dirk arched his lean body up to rub against Logan. He grabbed the slick, trying to open it without splurting it all over them. That he did was a miracle, an even bigger one that he got an appropriate amount on his fingers.

Dirk spread for him, legs going wide, knees drawing up. He didn't play; he fingerfucked Dirk, slicking his lover while he worked that half-erect prick.

It wasn't half-erect for long, especially after he found Dirk's gland, sliding his fingers over it. Dirk bucked, prick jerking to fill in his hand.

"Damn, that's so pretty." Dirk made his mouth dry. "Want in, baby."

"Yes, please." Dirk spread even wider, inviting him.

"Rubber?" He searched for a cover, groaning with frustration.

"Drawer. Drawer. My side," muttered Dirk, shifting restlessly beneath him.

"Right. Got it. Sorry." He groaned and found one, passed it to Dirk. "Glove me up."

"Making me do all the work." Dirk giggled softly, tearing at the package.

"That's me. I love your hands."

"You say the nicest things, love." Dirk got the condom out and in one hand while wrapping the other around his cock.

Logan whimpered softly, his head slamming back as he fought not to drive into Dirk's fingers. Luckily, Dirk didn't tease him, simply slid on the condom, then let him go.

"No more excuses. I need you inside me. Now."

Never let it be said he couldn't follow directions. He lined up and bared his teeth, groaning as he pressed into blazing heat.

"Oh God. Oh God. Oh God." Dirk reached for him, wrapped his hands around Logan's asscheeks and squeezed. "You feel so good. So fucking hot. God. Logan."

He nodded and drove in, gasping with pleasure. On his next thrust, Dirk bucked to meet him, body squeezing him tight.

"Love," he bit out. His thoughts shattered as he slammed their mouths together.

Dirk's sounds filled his mouth, Dirk's hands helping to bring him in. He filled Dirk over and over, the tight muscles dragging over his shaft.

It was so hot, so sexy. Then he looked up and met Dirk's eyes, and the love he saw there nearly sent him over the edge right then and there.

He found his soon-to-be husband a smile, a nod. He got it.

Dirk squeezed his ass tighter, fingers digging in. "Don't stop, Logan. Don't stop."

"Not. Won't. God, honey." He slammed in harder, driving in, deeper and deeper.

Dirk's body squeezed hard whenever Logan pulled out, trying to hold him in. He bent to drive back in, over and over, his need coiling inside him.

Dirk shone for him, eyes bright, body glistening with need. It was like he was seeing his lover for the first time all over again.

It was more than he could bear. "Soon."

"Yes." Dirk reached for his own cock, still holding on to Logan's ass with one hand. The other moved between them as Dirk jerked on his prick. The squeezes around Logan's prick got stronger, more intense.

All Logan could do was pant and try to hold on. His eyes crossed as he jerked, his hips moving furiously.

When Dirk came, Logan felt it on his cock, Dirk milking him strongly. Dirk's body demanded Logan's orgasm.

Thank God, because he was about to explode. He bit out a string of curse words before his balls let go.

Dirk groaned. "Such a filthy mouth you have, my dear."

"You were trying to kill me."

"No, I was trying to get you to make love to me. And it worked." Dirk's grin was happy—lazy and sated, but happy.

"Uh-huh. Didn't hurt you, did I?"

"No, I think what you did is the opposite of hurting."

"Excellent." He got rid of the condom and grabbed their pajama bottoms before he unlocked the door.

"And the best part of this whole thing might be this right here—you taking care of the door and pjs so I can lie here like a well-fucked lump."

Logan began to chuckle, tickled deep down.

"What? I meant it," Dirk protested. He was laughing, too, though.

"My butthead well-fucked lump."

"Oh, nice." Dirk threw a pillow at him, aim true and binging off his head.

He started laughing hard, heading over to tickle his lover. Dirk tried to crawl off the bed, but he wasn't quick enough, and Logan dug his fingers in, making Dirk buck and chortle.

They rolled together, ending in each other's arms, both of them panting. Dirk brought their mouths together for a quick kiss.

"I love you, Logan. Like, really."

"Good, because I love you." Dirk had helped him make a family.

Dirk smiled warmly and squeezed him in a hug. "Better get some sleep, love. Those babies of ours are going to be awake before you know it."

"Yeah. And we have a party. All our friends."

"Are you surprising me with a wedding tomorrow?"

"Nope. I'm just celebrating our engagement with burned meat." He rubbed their noses together. "Are you surprising me with a wedding tomorrow?"

"I didn't even know we were having our friends over until this evening, so no. Just friends and celebrating, eh?"

"Yeah. Us celebrating each other."

"That's cool. I'm guessing the girls might have an idea or forty to add to any wedding plans, eh?" Dirk hugged him closer. "Let's do it soon."

"As soon as we're ready."

"Well, we could wait until the triplets are old enough to participate," Dirk noted.

He pondered that. "We could. Or we could renew our vows in a few years...."

"Oh, I like that idea! To be honest, the thought of waiting three or four years doesn't really appeal. If we're going to do it, let's do it, huh?"

"Well, we can go get our license Monday." That would work. Then they could have Zack, who had done the course online so he could join another couple, marry them.

"Yeah? I'd like that. If it's what you want." Dirk could have this shyness about him at times.

"If it's what we want."

"Well, I do. I don't see a reason to wait now that the girls both know and that we're telling all our friends tomorrow. I want everyone to know I chose you and you chose me back." Dirk shifted, and Logan could feel the long cock against his thigh, filling slowly. "It makes me hot."

"I have a question for you, honey. Would you be willing to adopt the triplets?" Dirk was their parent as much as he was.

"Oh, Logan." Dirk hugged him tight, but he was pretty sure he saw tears gathering in Dirk's eyes before the hug. "Yes. Absolutely."

"Good." He held Dirk close. His babies were going to have a family. They were going to be a family.

Dirk held on just as hard. "I'm going to be thankful every day for the rest of my life that we are all going to be a real family together. Legal and everything."

"Melly always said they were her babies. From the start."

Dirk chuckled. "Yeah, she always has said that. She knew. Hey, you want to adopt her, too, right?"

"If she wants me to. Do you think she will?"

"I do. She loves you like she loves those babies."

"I'll ask her." He sobered, met Dirk's gaze. "You know that Sarah's nowhere near ready for a discussion about adoption. She may never be."

"I don't think I'd ever ask her, really. I'd let her know somehow it was on the table if she wanted it, but it'll have to come from her, and I'm okay if it never does. I will always be there for her, and I hope she knows that's true whether or not we're ever legally father and daughter."

His husband-to-be was a good man.

"I think she does. There is just so much changing in her life right now, she isn't capable of too much more."

"I know, love. And I wouldn't want her to think I was trying to replace her mother." Dirk squeezed him. "I'm going to do everything I can to make sure she feels welcome, that she knows she's a part of our family."

"Thank you. She needs that, to believe she's home and she's wanted."

"She is, Logan. You know she is. She's a beautiful, wonderful girl who is going to grow up to be an amazing woman. I swear we're going to make this work for every single one of us."

"We are. Our family. Our home. Our—"

"Da! Daddy Logan! I had a bad dream." Melly launched herself onto the bed and into his arms.

Dirk shifted, giving her room between them, but Dirk let him hold Melly, comfort her.

"Sh. Sh, it's okay. What did you dream?"

"A monster ate my babies! A bad monster."

"Did you want to go in and see them? You'll have to be very, very quiet if you do. We don't want to wake them."

She sniffled and nodded. "I need to make sure my babies are good."

"Well, come on, then. We'll make sure." He stood up with Melly in his arms. "Be right back, love."

Dirk smiled at him, looking so pleased. "I'll be here."

Melly held on to his neck, leaning her head against his shoulder, trusting him completely.

He opened the door to the nursery. The triplets were sleeping soundly. "See," he whispered. "All is well."

She leaned away from him to see better, then nodded. "My babies are okay." She wrapped her arms back around him, squeezing his neck. "Thank you, Daddy Logan."

"You're welcome, baby. You want to come to bed with us or your own bed?"

"I sleep with daddies."

"Okay." He carried her back to their bedroom where Dirk was waiting for them, looking half-asleep.

"Everyone good?" Dirk asked.

"Everyone is solid." He handed Mel over and crawled into the bed.

Mel settled in between them, and Dirk kissed the top of her head and then gave Logan a peck on the cheek. He'd no sooner turned the light off than another little voice sounded at the door.

"Daddy? I had a bad dream." Sarah sounded so very young.

"Did you?" He scooted over and held the blanket up. "Come lie down and keep me company."

She crawled into bed with him.

"Hi, Sarah," Mel whispered.

"Did you have a bad dream too?" Sarah asked.

"I dreamed a monster had the babies!"

"That's a terrible dream."

"I know! Daddy Logan showed me they were okay."

Sarah patted his shoulder. "You're a good daddy."

"I try." He smiled at her. "I love you, baby."

"Uh-huh. Me too."

"Me too!" added Mel.

"Yeah, me three." Dirk found his hand beneath the covers and twined their fingers together.

"Sleep, you three dorks. Barbecue tomorrow."

"You called me a dork, Daddy!" Sarah protested.

"He called us all dorks, honey, so you're in good company," Dirk noted.

"Uh-huh. Sh. Nighttime." Melly sighed and cuddled in.

"G'night baby girls. Night, love," Dirk murmured.

They all shifted and settled, and both girls were soon sound asleep.

This was all he wanted in the world. His family, together.

Chapter Eighteen

THE weather was gorgeous: warm, dry, and sunny.
They had put up a couple of canopies in the backyard
with tables holding goodies and drinks beneath the
shade they provided. The play structure and the
playhouse and kitchen were in full use, the kids having
a blast together.

The backyard was full of their friends. Dirk looked
around, smiling, feeling good. This was the family of
their hearts.

He wasn't sure how it had all happened, how it had
all been so good, but he was happy for it.

They were going to make the announcement about
them being engaged soon enough. They wanted to make
sure everyone was there first. The triplets were being
passed around, everyone wanting a turn with one of the

babies. He himself had baby Dylan fast asleep in his arms. Logan was supposed to be holding his godson, but had gotten a call or something.

It was fascinating, meeting Sarah's best friends for the first time, knowing that this was another new part of his life. So far the girls all seemed nice. It would be interesting to see how much they were willing to include Melly once Zack's girls and Aiden's oldest were gone. For now Melly and Linds were thick as thieves and not bothering the older girls at all.

He wasn't worried. If Sarah and her friends weren't interested in having Melly around, Dirk knew she would be more than happy to spend time with her babies.

Hell, he knew the guys would let Linds stay if he asked. Maybe they'd appreciate having a sleepover of their own. Maybe he'd wait and see how tired he and Logan were at the end of the day after everyone had left.

Dev wandered over with two cans of apple cider in hand. "I thought you might like some cider. And also a break from baby holding—I know you do that all the time with the triplets."

Dirk looked down at Dylan, who was all sleepy baby, and he shook his head. "No, I'm good."

"You know, I never thought he'd sleep. Ever."

"He knew you were worried, eh? And then you found Aiden, and you could both relax." Dirk knew that babies picked up on how the people around them were feeling. The triplets were little barometers for their family—sure to be fussy if any one of them was upset about something. It was intriguing, and he bet if he were the paper-writing type, he could wrangle a grant out of someone to do a study about it.

Unfortunately he was too busy raising three daughters and two sons to manage.

"So, this afternoon came out of the blue, didn't it?"

Dirk shrugged casually. He wasn't spilling the beans until Logan was ready to. He was pretty sure his husband-to-be had a speech prepared in his head, if not actually written down.

"It's a beautiful day, though," Dev added, "and there's enough food for an army."

That made Dirk laugh. "That's because even when we say you don't need to bring anything, you hooligans bring a ton anyway."

"Oh, I think it's a great spread. You want anything?"

"Did I see you guys brought tacos?" He totally might trade Dylan off for some food. His belly was grumbling at him, after all.

"We brought two dozen. Go get you some."

Dirk passed little Dylan to his daddy. "Thanks, dude." Then he headed toward the food tent where he'd seen the tacos. Melly came running over to show him the princess-colored piece of cake she'd found. Then she was off again, running to join Linds at the little kitchen.

Logan came out, laughing as Sarah and the older girls grabbed hot dogs. "Hey, babe."

He felt his smile blooming from his stomach. "Hey, Logan." He wrapped an arm around Logan's waist. "Having fun?"

"I am. Everyone seems to be having a good time, huh?"

"Uh-huh. You ready to let everyone know why they're here?" He was. He wanted to share the good news with their gang, who'd been here for the good and the bad.

"I am. Let's share our good news."

"Did you bring out the champagne?" He looked around to see if the glasses and fizzy wine were out.

"I got the acrylic flutes. I thought those were safe. Also, champagne and fizzy apple juice."

"So the girls can toast too. You think of everything." He gave Logan a kiss. "I'll make sure everyone has a glass."

"I'll do that." Zack appeared out of nowhere. "You two make your announcement."

Dirk laughed; he was unaccountably nervous. He took Logan's hand and squeezed, then cleared his throat to see if that would get everyone's attention.

When it didn't, Logan laughed. "Hey, guys. We have news!"

"Are you two having more babies?" someone said, and they all cracked up.

"You never know," Dirk said when everyone had quieted.

Melly put her hands on her hips. "No more babies, Da. Not until mine are big."

That had them all laughing again. God, he loved his daughter—he really did.

Logan grinned, one hand around Dirk's waist. "Dirk and I would like to announce that we're getting married!"

Cheers went up all around, and Zack raised his glass and opened his mouth.

"Your dad can't marry a boy," one of Sarah's friends announced, the pronouncement quite loud in the moment of quiet.

Sarah snorted. "Sure he can. Besides, Dirk isn't a boy. He's old."

Dirk's mouth dropped open and snapped closed in a matter of second. Then he opened it again but didn't know what to say. He felt like a guppy.

"Two men can absolutely get married," Zack said. "Or two women. Or a man and a woman. It doesn't matter who you love, just that you love them well." Zack turned back to the rest of them, raising his glass a little higher and segueing nicely into his toast. "And both Logan and Dirk have found love with each other. Let's all raise a glass to their engagement. I think it's a wonderful thing that they are going to make this piecemeal family into a legally bound one."

"Here, here!" Aiden cried. "Happy engagement, guys!"

Everybody lifted their glasses and took a drink, and Dirk turned to Logan, smiling with his whole face. In fact he was smiling so hard it almost hurt. They leaned together and shared a quick kiss.

"I love you," he whispered. "Thank you."

"No, thank you. I can't imagine my life without you now."

"Good thing you don't have to, hmm?"

"Yeah, a very good thing."

"Okay, you two, enough of being sappy." Dev grabbed his digital camera. "It's picture time."

"All of us, Da? All of us?" How could he tell that face no? Not that he wanted to, but this was telling him that his Melly girl would always have him wrapped around her little finger. Not that he'd have it any other way.

Dirk reached down and picked her up, settling her on his hip. "Of course all of us. We're going to be one big family, right?"

"Me and you and Sarah and my babies."

Logan gasped dramatically. "What about me?"

"You too, Daddy Logan."

There was a collective "aww" from their friends as Melly patted Logan's cheek.

"Thank you, my girl. I want to be in the pictures too."

She lunged for Logan, who caught her despite the surprise.

"Love you, my Melly girl. So much."

It made Dirk feel gooey inside to see how wonderful his husband-to-be was with his baby girl.

"I love you, Daddy Logan. Pictures!"

"Come on, Sarah." Dirk waved her over.

Sarah grabbed Seb, the guys bringing the other two.

In no time, they were all together, him and Logan, the girls, and their triplets, smiling for Dev and his camera. Their first family photos.

"Make sure we all get the pictures, Dev. These are great." Aiden gave them the thumbs-up over Dev's shoulder.

Everyone had their phones out, all taking their own versions.

Sarah got bored first. "Can I go play now?"

"Absolutely. Melly, go on, you too." Logan kissed Melly on the forehead.

Melly went running after Sarah and her friends, leaving all the grown-ups together, and Dirk was happy to hang out with everyone, to be close to Logan.

He rocked Suzy, laughing as she made faces at him. He made them back at her, delighted to have her laugh at him in return. God, he loved her. And her brothers. And their dad. How had he gotten so lucky?

"Are you having fun, honey?" Logan asked, a warm smile on his face.

"I am." How could he not? With his family and friends here, celebrating life with him? "How about you?"

"It's perfect. All of it."

He leaned against his lover, resting his head against Logan. "This is more than I ever dreamed, you know?"

He had a home, babies, a lover—it was magical.

"I'm just glad you kept trying to catch my attention." Logan winked at him. "I can be clueless."

"Well, and I think I was dorkily shy about it too. You were—are—this hot, studly lawyer. I was just a half-employed bum. Now I'm an unemployed bum, but I'm yours." And he was happier than he'd ever been.

"You're more than unemployed. You're raising our babies."

"Yeah, but it sounded more dramatic the way I said it."

Logan nodded. "True, but you can't denigrate yourself in front of our babies."

He cupped Logan's cheek, rubbing it with his thumb. "You make me feel like a million dollars."

"You two are basking. Come man the grill, man, and make burgers." Zack was all smiles.

"You do it," Dirk suggested. "I'll sit on the sidelines and admire your grilling prowess."

"Excellent idea. Admire my butt too."

"I always admire that." Dirk walked around Logan, nodding. "Yep. Always."

Zack threw up his hands. "Basking."

"Aren't we supposed to?" Logan asked. "It seems like the right thing to do."

"Yeah, I think it's in the handbook," Logan noted.

"And he's the lawyer—he knows about rules." Dirk smirked and admired his man.

"Absolutely. It's in section 5, clause 59. Basking is always allowed, but definitely during engagement parties."

Zack laughed and Dirk simply grinned. God, he loved Dirk.

Suzy began to fuss, catching his attention. "Someone needs her bottle."

"I've got her," Zack offered, taking her from his arms just like that. "You help that one get food going before we all starve to death."

Like there weren't eight million bowls and plates of munchies on the tables.

"On it." Logan bounced over the deck, beaming all the way.

Dirk found himself watching and grinning. Yeah, he was basking. He thought that was a really good thing.

Chapter Nineteen

LOGAN sat in the kitchen, snacking on leftovers and reliving their day. The house was full of kids and friends, food and laughter.

It was perfect.

His husband-to-be was on the couch, head against the back cushion, snoring as he held Seb and Sam against his chest. Suzy was in her swing, eyes open, watching everything.

Aiden came and sat next to him. "Hey, old friend."

"Hey, buddy. How're you?"

"I'm actually really good. It makes my heart glad to see the two of you so happy." Aiden leaned over to hug him. "Who knew Dirk would be the one for you? Although I have to admit, I did think he was mooning over you from when he first started coming to the group."

Logan blinked. Really? How cool. "I didn't notice. I just loved how he was with Melly."

"Yeah, you can tell a lot about a man by how he treats kids—his own and other people's. Dirk's one of the good ones. Oh, and thanks for having Linds over tonight. She's pretty excited about having her first big-girls' sleepover without either of her daddies. Of course, I may be making a trip back here at midnight if she suddenly decides that being here overnight without either of her daddies is scary."

"Are you sure you two don't want to stay in the blue room? You know you and the babies are welcome."

"That's so tempting. I'll talk to Dev. I imagine we'll take you up on that, if you're sure you want all the extra people after having a full day of guests."

"We'll make waffles in the morning, hmm? Have a lazy Sunday." He loved having a group of people around.

"That's sounds awesome. We're in." Aiden laughed and gave him a hug.

"Do you want the Pack 'n Play for your little ones?"

"That'd be perfect. We can keep them in the room with us and not worry about our babies waking your babies and vice versa." Aiden waved Dev over. "Hey, babe, we're all staying over. Logan has promised us waffles in the morning even."

Dev's smile widened. "That's awesome. I've already fielded a couple of questions from Linds that made me think she wasn't going to make it the whole night on her own, so this'll save one of us having to come back for her." Dev sat on the other side of Logan. "How can there be three of us sitting here with five babies between us and yet none of us is holding a single one of them?"

Aiden shook his head. "Don't look a gift horse in the mouth, babe."

"I'm not—it seems weird is all."

"If you need one, Suzy is happy to be picked up." He winked, playing with them. "Seriously, there's tons of room, and God knows we have enough food."

"Yeah, it's like you shopped for an army."

"There are a lot of young girls here," Dev noted. "Who from what I can see have never-ending bellies. So I think that equals an army."

"Right? They've already been down for snacks three times."

"Linds eats like a fiend every time she has a growth spurt," Aiden noted, Dev vigorously nodding his agreement.

"And there's a bunch of tweens trying to become young ladies." He rolled his eyes. "I'm going to have to buy stock in Doritos."

They were all laughing as Dirk came in, carrying all three triplets like it was the easiest thing in the world. "This looks like the fun room."

Logan held his arms out, Seb reaching for him. He took his little boy, snuggling him and laughing as he squealed.

"They're getting so big," Dev noted. "It's amazing how fast it happens."

Dev took Suzy, and Aiden took Sam. "You notice they didn't squeal for us like they did for Logan."

"Well, he's their daddy," Dirk said. "Aside from peekaboo, they love him best."

Logan thought maybe it was Melly who held that honor, but he wasn't going to argue the point. "I am." Being a daddy, it was what he was made for. He knew that now.

Dirk sat on the floor, grinning at the three of them on the couch. "I should find your camera, Dev. This is a great picture."

"Daddy? Can we have another snack?"

He looked to Dirk to take the baby, but Dirk hopped up and headed back to the kitchen to help the girls.

"What do you think they're feeding up there?" Dev asked as Sarah followed after Dirk.

"The monster under the bed," Aiden suggested.

"There's also the closet," Dev said.

"Oh God no. Have you seen that thing? No monsters would dare."

Returning from the kitchen, Dirk chuckled. "You forget that I know what your closet looks like, love. The apple doesn't fall very far from the tree."

"She's a gorgeous little messy apple, though…."

"Gorgeous and smart and a great big sister. And she and her friends got a big bottle of Orange Crush and three bags of chips. They are going to be up until Tuesday." Dirk laughed.

"Either that or they'll crash like lead balloons in the morning."

"I see the party is in here," noted Zack. "And most of the babies. Did you guys lose Bee and Dylan?"

"They're snuggled up together in that pile of blankets. Are your girls with Melly?"

"They are. They're watching *Coco* for the five millionth time."

"It'll be *Moana* next," Dirk noted. "Luckily I like them both as I can pretty much quote the entire movies verbatim."

"Would you like to give us a performance?" Aiden asked.

"No."

Logan began to chuckle. "At least it's not *Tangled*. Sarah watched that a thousand times."

"I've never seen that one." Dirk said it like it was a badge of honor. It probably was. If nothing else it proved that Dirk's girl was younger than his.

"That's a lucky break," Logan noted.

"Or a lucky braid," Zack teased.

Logan groaned. "That was very bad."

"I aim to please." Zack looked utterly unrepentant.

If Zack hadn't been holding one of the triplets, Logan would have thrown a pillow or something at him.

The others were all laughing, except for Dirk. "Am I missing a joke?"

"Yeah, baby, you are. A bad one. Just be grateful you don't get it."

"Okay." Dirk came and pushed between him and Aiden to lean against him. Seb wiggled and cooed, drawing Dirk's attention. "Hello, son. Are you enjoying daddy time? Are you?" Dirk made all sorts of faces, making Seb laugh.

He looked at the guys. "No one makes them laugh like Dirk."

"That's 'cause I make the best idiotic faces."

"Totally." He leaned to get a kiss. "Never change."

"I'll try not to." Dirk closed the distance between their lips, and they lingered together.

Dev and Aiden "awwed" in unison.

"Save some for the wedding," teased Zack.

"Have you picked a date yet?" Dev asked.

"We're going to go get the license Monday. We're not doing a big church wedding or anything."

"You have to invite us! Otherwise you won't get babysitters for your honeymoon night." Aiden was a butthead.

"When's the next Teddy Bear Club day?" Dirk asked.

"You mean Tuesday?"

"Yeah. How about that?"

Logan smiled. It would be a lovely place for a wedding.

"We were going to ask Zack to marry us, anyway, right? You could take Sarah out of school for the day so she can be there too." Dirk smiled at him.

"It's perfect. We'll have a ceremony with our best friends and all the kids." He couldn't think of anything better.

"That works for me." Dirk beamed at him.

And if they had it the coming Tuesday, there wouldn't be a chance for any of the crazy wedding accoutrements that turned people into groomzillas and cost a fortune.

They didn't need the tuxes, the several hundred people, the pomp and circumstance. They didn't even need a city hall wedding. They needed exactly what this would be. A Teddy Bear Club wedding.

"Zack?" he asked. "How does that work for you?"

"I'll have to make sure I have someone to cover the cash register for me for the rest of the day, but yeah, that works for me. I'll be honored to both host and officiate."

"Perfect. Let's do it, then. Tuesday it is."

Aiden and Dev cheered. Dirk just beamed at him, looking so pleased.

"Shortest engagement in history."

"We're too busy for a long engagement," Dirk suggested.

"You know it." He grabbed Dirk in his free arm and kissed him, hard.

Groaning, Dirk matched his passion. "I do love you."

"Eww, Daddy!" Sarah stared at him wide-eyed. "No kissing! Ice cream?"

"More food?" Hadn't Dirk just sent her back with a couple bags of chips?

"We're hungry!"

"Okay, okay." He passed Seb over to his husband-to-be, stole another kiss, and stood. He grabbed his daughter's hand and let her lead him to the kitchen. "So you want cones or sundaes?"

"Milkshakes, Daddy? Please? You make the best ones."

"You got it, honey." He grabbed the ice cream and the milk and set them on the counter by the blender. "Are you and your friends having a good time?"

"Uh-huh. They picked a scary movie to watch."

Was that why she kept coming down for food? "Are you okay with that?" Hell, were the rest of them okay with that—a bunch of nine- and ten-year-old girls might not all want to watch something scary, but if one suggested it, the rest might feel the need to do it even if they didn't want to. He might not be a kid anymore, but he could remember what peer pressure was like.

She shook her head, but she said, "I guess so?"

"Did everyone want to watch the scary movie?" Did he need to go up and make sure they were okay? He was pretty sure he did. He'd help Sarah carry the milkshakes up to her room and suss out the situation.

"I-I guess so?"

"Let's go upstairs, okay? I'll help get the shakes up there." He thought maybe they needed to talk about what daddies thought scary was.

He got them made, and up they went, Sarah with two of the milkshakes, and he had the other three.

"Are you having a good party, Daddy?" She took the stairs a little slowly, and he could tell she was stretching out her trip.

"I am. It's a happy occasion. What about you, honey? Are you having a good party with your posse?" He deliberately used a word that had earned him laughter the day before.

"Yeah. It's been fun to run around."

"I'm glad, honey." It was the first big sleepover he'd hosted for her ever, and he did want it to go well.

"I just... ghosts... do you think Mommy is a ghost?"

Oh, crap, what were they watching? "No, Sarah. I believe your mother went to heaven."

"Me too. I don't want her to be a ghost." There were tears right under the surface.

"She's not a ghost, honey, she's an angel, and she's looking out for you, okay?" He needed to change the channel on whatever they were watching. "Come on, these milkshakes are melting."

"Right. Daddy?" She caught his eyes. "Please don't let them know I'm scared."

"Your secret is safe with me, sweetie." He was going to tell them scary movies were for older girls. He could totally pretend he'd just come up with the milkshakes and was completely surprised by what they were watching.

They went into Sarah's room.

Poltergeist was on the screen, one of the girls hiding under a blanket, another with tears on her cheeks.

"Holy Fu-udgsicles. What are you girls watching?" He went over to the TV and turned it off, figuring that would be quicker than trying to find the remote. "Whose idea was it to watch this?"

"It's PG-13! It said so, Mr. Bartram. I promise!" Belinda looked at him, wide-eyed.

"Well, the last time I looked, at least, none of you is thirteen yet. And this one is very scary. I'm not comfortable with you watching it." He turned the overhead light on and set his tray of milkshakes on the table. "Does anyone need a hug?" Even Belinda didn't look like she'd been happy watching the movie.

The girls all came to him, getting a hug and a milkshake, one at a time.

Sarah was last, and she threw her arms around his neck. "You're the best daddy," she whispered.

"I love you too, baby girl. How about *The Incredibles*?"

A chorus of "yays" went up, and Logan found the remote and cued up the movie.

"This is one of my favorites—do you mind if I watch a bit of it with you?" Logan wasn't going to walk out and let the girls have trouble again.

They all agreed he could, and he sat on one side of the bed, his back against the headboard. "You gonna share your milkshake, Miss Sarah?"

"Yeah, Daddy." He doubted Sarah was hungry at all.

"Thank you." He had a few mouthfuls. It was good if he did say so himself. Then he focused on the movie. This was one that he enjoyed, and hopefully it would turn things around for the girls. At least it was early in the evening and not the middle of the night that they'd gone for the scary movie. By the time it was really late, he hoped the happy stuff would have overcome the scary.

When Dirk came up to check on him, the girls had played beauty shop with him, the little girls giggling happily as they painted his nails and lips.

Dirk smirked, and Logan was pretty sure Dirk was trying hard not to laugh. "Wow. You are looking very pretty." He whipped his phone out. "In fact, this should be shared."

Logan's eyes went wide, and he shook his head. Oh no. There was no reason to record this for posterity.

Dirk took five or six photos. "Oh yeah."

"Girls. I think Dirk needs a makeover. Don't you?"

Dirk took a step back. "I don't know about that."

The girls knew, though, swarming Dirk.

He leaned back and let his nails dry, knowing that Dirk didn't know about all of this. Yet.

"You sit here, Uncle Dirk." Sarah showed Dirk to the "salon" chair.

"Okay." Dirk shot him a look but then gave the girls a smile. "So what do I need to do?"

"You just sit there," Belinda informed him. "We do all the work."

Logan fought the urge to laugh. Instead, he texted the guys. *Beauty makeover time. Will be down soonish. pictures!*

Logan shook his head. Oh, he was taking pictures of Dirk, but that was for the two of them and Sarah and Mel. He knew Dirk wouldn't share the ones he'd taken of Logan if he didn't share the ones he was about to take of Dirk.

This was for them to look back on and laugh, all seven of them.

Dirk was a good sport, making fishy faces and closing his eyes when told to.

By the time they were done, none of them could possibly keep their laughter in.

Mel, Linds, and Zack's girls had come up to join in the fun, too, the room a gaggle of happy girls. He was pretty sure the scary movie incident had passed, and everyone was happy to come down to the media center and snuggle in the big chairs to watch *Beauty and the Beast* on the big screen.

Once they had them all set up and watching, he and Dirk were able to finally head back to their guests. Which turned out to be just Zack, Aiden, and Dev, everyone else having made their way home.

They all plopped down, the five infants all on blankets on the floor.

"You guys both look very, uh... beautiful?"

"You should have seen us before we washed our faces." Dirk shook his head. "The girls had such fun doing it."

"There is a lot of laughing going on," Aiden said. "Are they all watching cartoons now?"

"They are. Sarah's got Linds and Mel in her chair."

"I'm glad you guys stayed." Dirk headed toward the kitchen. "Can I get anyone anything?"

"Can I have a Coke, love?"

"You can have anything you want."

"I already do."

Dirk's expression went soft, and the guys all went "aww."

Yeah, it was a sappy moment—sue them.

They deserved a little sap, just because.

"Anybody else want anything?" Dirk asked. "Just so you know, food and drink are all I'm offering the rest of you hooligans."

Zack laughed. "I should probably get my girls and head home."

"Why don't you all stay as well—I've heard someone is making waffles for breakfast, and we've got more than enough rooms with beds." Dirk met Logan's eyes, smiling.

"Please. The girls are happy, and they've already had showers and are in their pjs." Logan loved how everyone had planned for tired, dirty kids who needed baths.

"Well, okay, then. I might need to borrow someone's sweats to sleep in…."

"Actually, I was going to make a quick run back to our place to grab pajamas for Aiden and me—you could join and pick up anything else you or the girls need," Dev suggested.

"You two okay with everyone?" Zack asked.

"Us and—" He did a quick calculation. "—fourteen kids? No problem."

"Hey, I'm staying here too," Aiden protested. "So us three and fourteen kids—the odds are suddenly much, much better."

Dirk cackled. "Hurry. We've got another forty-five minutes before that movie ends and they start moving again."

"You guys holler if you want us to grab anything on the way," Dev said, and Logan cracked up.

"Because we don't have enough food."

"Possibly we don't," Dirk noted. "I think the girls snagged the last bag of chips. We're getting pizza in a while, though, so I think we're fine. Thanks, though."

"Okay. We're out of here." Dev headed out with Zack.

Dirk sat with Logan and Aiden, his face wreathed in a smile. "We're never ever going to be bored again."

"No, I imagine not." Logan didn't think that was a bad thing.

Aiden snorted. "Nope. Because you know once the youngest are ready to head out into the world on their own, the older ones will be bringing your grandbabies home."

"I will hurt you, man." No talking about grandbabies. None.

"Hey, it's not my fault you wound up with five kids. Even if some of them don't have kids, odds are you'll wind up with several grandkids. Hell, if they all have kids, that's five at the very least. And if they follow your guys' example, it'll be closer to twenty-five grandkids."

Dirk flipped Aiden off. "Hush now."

Twenty-five grandbabies....

God. He was going to pass out.

Aiden nearly choked on his own laughter.

Dirk touched Logan's shoulder. "Hey. We have five kids, three of whom are babies, and the house is currently full of God knows how many girls under thirteen. We need to worry about the next twelve hours. Trust me, the next twelve years will take care of themselves. So will the twelve after that."

"Yeah, yeah. You know how many billable hours I'll need, love?"

"Sh. Right now all you have to worry about is how you're going to get the glitter out of your hair and the rest of that gloss off your lips." Dirk kissed him. "I'm serious. Don't miss out on today because you're worrying about tomorrow. I'm pretty sure there's all sorts of smart-sounding proverbs about that, but of course none of them are coming to mind at the moment."

"Uh-huh. Good thing you'll be raising our babies so you can proverbize them."

"Proverbize?" Dirk snorted. "I love it."

"You're no fun, Dirk." Aiden pouted in Dirk's direction. "I had him going with that twenty-five grandkids thing."

"I think that will be magical," Dirk said. "When it happens."

Logan stared at Dirk. "Really?"

"Like I said, babe, it's forever from now. Focus on our little girls and babies."

Right on cue, Logan's godson turned his head and reached for him. "Unca."

"Oh. Hey, baby." He slid down on the floor and wrapped Dylan in his arms. "Did you guys hear that?"

"Oh my God, did we?" Dirk was bouncing. "He said your name!"

"Damn." Aiden shook his head. "Dev is going to be so sad he missed this."

"Get your phone. What if he does it again?" Logan couldn't believe it. "Hey, baby boy. Say my name. Say Uncle Logan."

"Has he said Dada yet?" Dirk asked.

"No! His first word was you, Logan." Aiden grabbed his phone and trained it on him and Dylan. "Say it again, baby D. Say Unca."

Dirk laughed. "Shouldn't you be encouraging him to say 'Dada'?"

"Not without Dev here. Not a chance."

"Heh, you've got a point," Dirk conceded. "Okay, then. Hey, Dylan. Can you say it again? Can you say un-ca?"

"Come on, baby." He rubbed noses with Dylan, and the baby squealed, grabbing his ears.

"Un-ca!"

"Whoo! Did you get it?" Dirk asked.

"Yeah. Yeah, I did." Aiden laughed. "Do it again, Dylan."

"Un-ca! Un-ca! Un-ca!"

Logan hugged his godson tight. "Dy-lan! Dy-lan! Dy-lan!"

"Un-ca!"

Dirk and Aiden were both laughing, cheering.

All the babies began to wake, Sebastian beginning to cry as Suzy popped him in the nose.

Still laughing, Dirk leaned over the boys and undid them from their blanket cocoons. He started to pull faces at them and touch them. God, his almost husband was good with the babies.

Bee went right to her father. "Dada!"

Aiden picked her up and bounced her on his leg, chattering away at her.

"Un-ca!" Dylan pronounced, slapping his cheeks again.

Logan laughed and grabbed one hand, blowing a raspberry against Dylan's fat little palm, making his godson squeal with delight.

God, they were lucky bastards.

Chapter Twenty

HE was getting married today. Dirk repeated the words in his head a few times. Not only was he getting married today, he was marrying the man he loved. The man he'd been in love with for a while now. He had his friends and his kids around him to witness and celebrate.

Grinning, he took the flowers Melly had picked from the garden and held them like a bouquet. He was wearing a pair of good slacks and a light blue dress shirt. He knew he looked good. But not as good as Logan.

Logan was in a dove-gray shirt, one that showed his physique. It was the smile, though. That was what made his lover, his soon-to-be husband, so beautiful.

He took Logan's hand, and they walked together to where Zack was standing.

Aiden and Dev had the triplets, while Melly and Sarah stood with Zack, waiting to stand with their daddies.

Logan smiled at him. "You ready for this, honey?"

He didn't even need to think about it. "Yeah, I really am."

"Me too." Logan beamed, bright and happy. "Let's go get married."

"Yeah, let's."

They made their way to where Zack and the girls stood. Zack had a warm smile for them, and Melly bounced and squealed. She grabbed Dirk's hand, squeezed it.

"Da. You're getting married!"

"I am. Are you going to say yes when Uncle Zack asks you if you want to be a part of this new family?" They'd decided that both older girls deserved to be a part of their ceremony, of the I dos.

"Uh-huh. My sissy and my babies and Da and Daddy Logan."

"Yeah, that's right." He loved Logan, but on top of that, Melly was getting another father, a big sister, and those babies of her as brothers and sister. Their life was so much richer now.

"What about you, Sarah?" he asked.

"We'll see." She winked at him, then hugged him tight. "It'll be okay, Da. I promise."

"Oh. Yeah, it will." She'd called him Da. He hugged her back. "It totally will."

He met Logan's eyes over her head, and his soon-to-be husband was all misty.

He stood, and they gathered around Zack. "We're ready."

"I'd say so. I can't think of a family that's more ready." Zack cleared his throat, offered them all a happy smile. "Dearly beloved, we are gathered together to celebrate the union of our dear friends, Dirk and Logan."

Melly bounced. "And Melly and Sarah and the babies!"

"Yes, sweetheart. And Melly and Sarah and the babies."

Dirk beamed at Zack. Then at Logan and at their girls. They were doing this right.

They were creating their family.

Coming in July 2019

Dreamspun Desires #85
Come Back Around by BA Tortuga
Leaning N

Can two divorced dads get a second chance at a redneck wedding?

When Reid Porter agrees to be his best friend's man of honor, he never considers that his ex, Mateo, will be there too. Which is ridiculous, because Jennifer is marrying Mat's brother. Reid would never let Jen down, though, so he finds himself at the Leaning N Ranch with his two daughters and a whole lot of baggage about seeing Mat again.

Mat loves his baby brother and would do anything for him, including face the love of his life, whom he's sure has moved on. When he and Reid come face-to-face after more than two years apart, they realize they've never let go. Now they have to do what they never could before—balance work, home, and children, while finding a way to come back around to each other's love.

Dreamspun Desires #86
Warm Heart by Amy Lane

Survive the adventure. Live to love.

Following a family emergency, snowboarder Tevyn Moore and financier Mallory Armstrong leave Donner Pass in a blizzard… and barely survive the helicopter crash that follows. Stranded with few supplies and no shelter, Tevyn and Mallory—and their injured pilot—are forced to rely on each other.

The mountain leaves no room for evasion, and Tevyn and Mal must confront the feelings that have been brewing between them for the past five years. Mallory has seen Tevyn through injury and victory. Can Tevyn see that Mallory's love is real?

Mallory's job is risk assessment. Tevyn's job is full-on risk. But to stay alive, Mallory needs to take some gambles and Tevyn needs to have faith in someone besides himself. Can the bond they discover on the mountain see them to rescue and beyond?